Pipeline

Brenda Adcock

Quest Books

Nederland, Texas

ISBN 978-1-932300-64-2

First Printing 2006

9 8 7 6 5 4 3 2 1

Cover design by Donna Pawlowski

Published by:

Regal Crest Enterprises, LLC
4700 Highway 365, Suite A
PMB 210
Port Arthur, Texas 77642

Find us on the World Wide Web at
http://www.regalcrest.biz

Printed in the United States of America

Acknowledgments

Writing can be a lonely undertaking and yet no one truly writes alone. Without the encouragement of my friends and family my dream could never have come true. There were many times when I wanted to quit. I wish to thank my best friend, Ron Whiteis, whose gift for seeing the "big picture" is amazing. My sincerest gratitude goes to Cathy LeNoir for taking a chance and allowing my characters to tell their story. I was blessed with two wonderful editors, Christi Cassidy and Susan Fabian, who pointed out my mistakes and made editing a painless learning process. Last, but never least, my special thanks to Cheryl for her patience and understanding. Who could ask for anything more?

To Cheryl –

The day you stepped into my life you made it worth living again.
I love you.

Chapter
One

AS I SWUNG my Blazer onto State Highway 783 toward San Antonio, I could still hear Cate's voice.

"Kyle's been shot."

Her words had jarred the serenity of a life I had finally begun to adjust to and dredged up memories I thought were safely tucked away in the deepest recesses of my mind.

It had begun as a perfect day. Jack, my seventeen-hand bay gelding, had been a perfect gentleman, wading into gently flowing low-water crossings, pausing for a drink while I let the heat from the sun pour over my face as I watched red-tailed hawks soar lazily over the cliffs rising from the banks of the Guadalupe River. I needed this calm...this peace. In my own mind, I hadn't changed over the years. But when I caught a glimpse of myself in a mirror, the face reflected there clearly showed that thirty years as a photojournalist, traveling endlessly to capture the tragedies human beings inflicted on one another, had taken their toll on me. Thank God for the genes I inherited from my parents. Without them I could have easily looked like the sad, defeated women I had photographed hundreds of times in Kosovo, Mexico, and Rwanda—their youth and their lives shattered by the events swirling around them over which they had no control. I knew I was older, a little past my mid-fifties, but my short, brunette hair was relatively free of gray, and I had managed to remain physically fit. There were times when I saw my reflection in a window and thought, not bad for a woman my age. Of course, there had been other times when I hardly recognized myself, expecting to see that much younger woman who still resided in my mind.

My philosophy on living had never changed. When something is over, it's just over. I had never looked back to think about what I had left behind. My approach had always been to simply walk away, accepting the finality of each situation once I had made my decision. When I was in my twenties, I couldn't wait to leave this peaceful place, so I turned my back on it all and walked away. No regrets. Regrets for what I left behind served no purpose. What I didn't know when I was twenty-five was that there would always be regrets, no matter how far or how fast you tried to walk away.

Halfway back to my house I could feel Jack's muscles beginning to bunch, and it took all the strength I had to hold him in check until we reached the edge of the long green meadow that stretched for nearly a mile before my house came into view. Still holding back the reins as Jack pranced in anticipation, I leaned forward and stroked his neck as I whispered in his ear, "Run like the wind, Jack." I loosened the reins and felt his powerful rear leg muscles propel him forward. He ran flat out, rejoicing in the sheer exhilaration of running free.

His long stride was smooth as he covered yards at a time. The wind blew through my short hair, and I laughed out loud, enjoying my freedom as much as Jack. As we topped the last rise leading back to home, I caught a glimpse of a car I didn't recognize parked next to my housekeeper's car on the lawn in front of the house. Even as far away as we were, I could make out Lena pointing in my direction but couldn't tell anything about the person standing on the porch with her.

Jack slowed as we reached the corral next to the barn. He was lathered up and breathing heavily as I turned him toward the house. The visitor on the porch stepped into the sunlight as we approached, and I felt my heart rate increase when I saw her. Almost fifteen years had passed since I'd last seen her, but from a distance it didn't seem that she had changed at all.

I reined Jack to a stop as she came down the porch steps toward us. The sun highlighted her shoulder-length light brown hair, and when her eyes met mine they were the same deep blue I remembered. She was still a trim five foot seven and looked damn good for a woman of fifty. I allowed myself the luxury of visually scanning her from head to toe. Hidden beneath her slacks and loose-fitting, man-tailored shirt was a body that had never failed to drive me crazy with desire. The corners of my mouth began to form a smile, and I looked away from her as I realized my nipples were hardening with an arousal I hadn't felt in a very long time. She was stunning.

"Nice car," I said casually as I swung my right leg over the saddle horn and slid off the saddle.

"It's good to see you again too, Joanna." She never used my full name unless she was pissed. As soon as she set her jaw and shot me that cold look, I was instantly reminded of all the reasons I had walked away from her in spite of my physical desire to feel her smooth and sensuous body pressed against mine one more time. So much for a perfect fucking day.

Pulling Jack's reins over his head, I said, "Been a long time, Cate."

It had been too long, and small talk had never been my strong suit. Cate glanced over her shoulder at Lena, who was smoking what I guessed was probably her twentieth cigarette of the day as she leaned against the porch railing.

"Is there some place we can speak privately?" Cate asked.

"Sure." I shrugged. "Give me a few minutes to get this saddle off Jack."

"Lena," I called. "Show Ms. Hammond into my office, will you?"

Lena nodded and flicked her cigarette into a flowerbed under the porch as I led Jack toward the barn, wondering why Cate had suddenly made a reappearance in my now calm life.

Nearly twenty minutes later I brushed hay from my clothes and entered my house. Stopping in the kitchen to grab a drink, I asked Lena, "How long has she been here?"

"Maybe twenty, thirty minutes b'fore you get here." Lena shrugged. "She a bill collector or sumpthin'?"

"I wish," I muttered as I went toward my office.

When I entered the office, Cate was looking out the window, her arms crossed in front of her. She turned as I walked behind my desk and plopped down in the office chair.

"What can I do for you, Cate?" I asked as I sipped on a glass of sweet tea.

Still standing, she looked at me and said, "Kyle's been shot."

"What?" I set my glass down before my hand began shaking.

"It happened early yesterday evening..." her voice cracked.

I got up and moved toward her, unsure what to do next. "Is he..." I started weakly.

"He's alive," Cate answered as a tear escaped her eye and traveled down her cheek.

"Thank God!" I breathed. "Do the police know who shot him or why?"

"They've apprehended someone but have no idea why."

"I appreciate you coming here, Cate. But you could have called."

"I didn't think this was something I should tell you about our son over the phone," she said as her eyes shot up to mine and hardened slightly. I knew I should have taken her in my arms to comfort her, but somehow I wouldn't allow myself to get that close to her again.

"Is there anything I can do?"

Cate crossed the office and sat down on a rocker in front of my desk. "I drove to San Antonio last night as soon as I was notified. Kyle has a girlfriend, Sarita Ramirez. She said something odd while we were waiting for him to come out of surgery."

Returning to my chair, I leaned my elbows on the desk. "What did she say?"

"She was rambling quite a bit and was obviously upset, but she kept insisting his shooting was her fault," Cate said.

"What exactly did she say?"

"That she knew this would happen. I have no idea what she meant. When I asked her about it she would only say it was about a story he was researching."

"Which was?" I pressed, beginning to tire of having to drag every iota of information out of her.

"I don't know, and she wouldn't talk about it anymore. When I was alone with Kyle this morning I asked him what story he was working on, but he just said it wasn't related to his shooting. Then he told me not to worry."

"A little too late for that," I said with a slight chuckle.

Leaning forward in the rocker, Cate asked, "Would there be any chance you could come to San Antonio to see what you can find out?"

"Sounds to me like he doesn't want any help. And he

sure as shit wouldn't want any from me."

"He was hurt when you left, Jo," Cate said.

"The way I recall it," I frowned, "I was asked not to return."

Cate pushed herself out of the rocker and looked at the floor for a moment before looking at me again. "Well, I wanted to let you know about Kyle. I'd better get back to San Antonio before it gets any later."

As she turned to leave, I rose from my chair to escort her back to her car. She slipped her sunglasses on as we approached her car. I reached around her and opened the car door for her. "Have a safe trip," I said.

Although I couldn't see her eyes as she stepped into the car and looked up at me, I knew I had disappointed her the way I had so many times in the past.

"It was good to see you again, Jo."

I nodded and closed the door as she started the ignition. I stood with my hands in my jeans pockets as she backed away and turned to drive down the gravel road and out of my life...again. Regret. What a bitch that can be.

Lena was leaning against the doorframe, a cigarette dangling from the side of her mouth as I trudged slowly up the front steps.

"That you ex?" she asked.

"Yeah," I answered as I glanced over my shoulder and watched the dust kicked up by Cate's car dissipate.

Chapter
Two

THE MORNING AFTER Cate's unexpected visit, and a night of fitful sleep filled with nightmares and pleasant memories that merged incoherently, I carried a cup of coffee into my office and dug through the drawers in my desk until I found my address book. It was as old and beaten up as I was, but I hoped the numbers were still good. Thumbing through the pages I found the name I was looking for, punched in the number, and leaned back in my chair, holding the receiver against my ear with my shoulder. A few rings later a woman's voice answered.

"San Antonio Express."

"Frank Escobedo, please."

"One moment and I'll connect you."

The Express was one of those companies that had adopted Muzak for its phone system to entertain customers on hold. Streisand cooed one of her bigger hits into the headset. I liked the song, and it made the wait tolerable. At least it was better than that crap that passed for music these days. In the middle of a line, the music stopped abruptly.

"Escobedo," a familiar voice said.

"Frank," I said. "Joanna Carlisle."

"Jo!" he said with surprise in his voice. "I heard you was dead."

"Yeah, I heard that rumor, too." I smiled.

"Where the hell are you?"

"I'm back at the ranch outside Kerrville. Listen, Frank, I need a favor."

"So what else is new?" He laughed. "What'cha need this time?"

"My kid is a reporter in San Antonio, and apparently he's gotten himself into a little trouble. I need to find out what he's working on."

My kid. The words sounded funny to me now. He hadn't been my kid for a long time. I had given all that up by making a decision. Whether it had been right or wrong didn't really matter now. It had seemed like the only decision at the time.

"He a reporter for the Express?" Frank asked.

"The Light."

"You let your kid work for that rag?" He snorted.

"We're not exactly close. Someone shot him, and his mother asked me to look into it. See what you can find out, will you?"

"What's your kid's name?"

"Kyle Hammond."

"Think I saw a news flash come across the desk about that shootin'. What hospital is he at?"

"Hell, I don't know. You're a fuckin' reporter, find out."

"You want me to call when and if I find somethin'?"

"No, I'm coming to the city tomorrow. I'll swing by your office."

"I bought the last time, Jo."

"I remember. This one's on me, and if you find out anything useful, so's the next one."

He laughed. "Damn, it's good to hear your voice again, gal. See ya tomorrow."

IT WAS SHORTLY after noon, two days after Cate's visit, when I pulled into the visitor's section of the San Antonio Express parking lot. Early in my career I had sold a few pictures to the Express. Mostly guts and gore traffic stuff. The more gore and guts the better back then.

The receptionist at the front desk gave me directions to Frank's desk, and by the time the elevator door opened into the second floor newsroom, I was feeling at home in familiar surroundings. Frank Escobedo was a made-for-the-movies news reporter, craggy-faced with white shirt sleeves rolled halfway up his arms and tie hanging loosely around his neck. All the veteran reporters I have ever known had the same hairstyle, combed by running fingers through it while they talked on the phone chasing down tips and ferreting out information.

Frank saw me before I saw him and half stood to motion

me toward his desk. He was on the phone, scribbling notes, as I reached his desk. I sat down, resting my feet on an open lower desk drawer. The ashtray on Frank's desk was overflowing. It looked like a four-pack day already, and it was only lunchtime. He held out the pack of cigarettes to me as he jammed another one between his lips and lit it with the remains of his last cigarette. I shook my head, and he dropped the pack back on his desk. He stopped writing and rubbed his eyes.

"That's not very helpful, Tutti. What do you mean by 'some guys'? How many? Who are they? Everybody's got a name, stupid."

He listened for another second or two before interrupting whoever Tutti was.

"No! Now you wait just one good goddamn minute, you fuckin' hairball. You know the deal. No info, no dough. I don't give a shit what you think. I pay you for facts, and I ain't hearin' any. So unless you're plannin' to kick whatever it is you're usin' these days cold turkey, you better get your ass movin' and come up with somethin' more than 'these guys said.' Call me when you can do that. Otherwise don't waste my time."

Frank slammed the receiver down and rubbed his face again.

"Fuckin' junkies," he mumbled.

"I see you still have a way with people, Frank."

"Get your damn feet off my desk, Jo. Does this look like your living room?"

"Have you found out anything for me yet?" I asked as I sat up in the chair and got down to business.

"Yeah, a little," he said, exhaling loudly. "That asshole on the phone was an informant of mine. He knows some nasty folks and might find out something, depending on whether or not he can get money for his next fix from anyone else but me. The kid's in a private room over at Santa Rosa Medical Center. Got shot twice, but nothing vital was hit. He'll still be able to walk, talk, eat, fuck his girlfriend, but he'll be out of commission a week or two, dependin' on how tough he is. The cops arrested some kid, ten or eleven years old, who was the shooter, but undoubtedly, it wasn't his idea. They found a couple hundred bucks on him, so somebody probably hired him to do it. Nobody ever suspects a kid like that, and if his hands hadn't been shakin' so damn bad, your kid would be lyin' on a slab in the morgue instead of a hospital bed."

"Anything about a story he's supposed to be working on?"

"I tried to get in to see him last night. You know, *mano a mano*, but no go. I slipped a nurse a twenty to find out what she could, but it wasn't much. According to the nurse, he was pretty dopey from painkillers and sedatives but did say something about illegals."

"So what, Frank? Stories about illegals are a dime a dozen around this state."

The border between Texas and Mexico has never been your basic secure area. An illegal with the IQ of an armadillo could get across the border.

Texas lawmakers didn't have the guts to put a stop to the flow of illegals. Growers in the Valley needed workers to care for and harvest their crops, and illegals were a hell of a lot cheaper than legal workers. The state could impose hefty monetary penalties on the growers for hiring illegals, but that meant a rise in the prices of Valley produce, and consumers would be pissed if the price of their morning grapefruit doubled or tripled. Consumers didn't give a damn if the illegals earned twenty-five cents a day and lived in shitholes or if they worked twenty hours a day. They just wanted cheap produce.

"Maybe somewhere along the way he tripped onto something bigger." Frank shrugged. "Hell, maybe whatever he's doin' ain't even related to illegals. Could be anything, Jo."

I looked at the ceiling and took a deep breath. "Anything else?"

Frank flipped through his notepad and scanned each page.

"The only other thing the nurse told me was that the kid has only had two visitors since he's been in the hospital. One, I presume, is his mother, who the nurse described as...let me see...yeah, here, 'classy and probably rich.' She had him moved out of the ward and into a private room yesterday."

"Who's the other visitor?"

"Uh...a younger woman who she thinks is his girlfriend. Sarita Ramirez. The nurse tried to talk to her, too, but didn't get much except 'I warned him this would happen.' And that, my friend, is all I got."

"Sounds like this Sarita might know something."

"Well, you know how pillow talk is, Jo. After you're through rockin' the mattress, you can either fall asleep, raid the refrigerator, smoke a cigarette, or talk," Frank grinned.

"Or sometimes a combination of those choices." I smiled. "Well, come on. I'm buying." I stood up and rearranged my jeans.

He grabbed his jacket from the back of his chair. "I already called, and there'll be enchiladas and Corona Lights with a twist of lime waitin' by the time we get there."

Chapter
Three

SANTA ROSA MEDICAL Center is a large teaching hospital located between the interstate and downtown San Antonio, and it took me a while to find a parking place within reasonable walking distance. From the look of the people wandering in and out of the main entrance, the bulk of their customers appeared to be either indigent or heavily dependent on the Medicaid/Medicare program.

According to Frank, Kyle was in Room 515, a private suite. I hate hospitals, having spent my fair share of time in a variety of foreign and military field hospitals during my career, with the requisite scars to prove it. Whether it's a modern facility like this one or some olive drab tent in the middle of the desert, they all smell the same. The only difference is air conditioning or lack of it, but nothing can overwhelm the antiseptic smell. I followed an arrow that pointed toward Rooms 500-525 and, midway down the corridor, found a nurses' station where a young Hispanic woman who looked like a volunteer manned the desk. She smiled as I approached.

"Hello," I said. "Can you tell me how Kyle Hammond is?"

"Are you a family member or friend of the family?" the young woman asked pleasantly.

"A friend," I lied.

"I can't release information to anyone other than a family member, but I believe his mother is here. Would you like to speak to her?"

"Yeah, please."

"Who should I say is here?"

"Just tell her a friend from Kerrville." I smiled. "I'll be in the waiting room."

She disappeared from the desk, and I made my way to the

waiting room. I was watching a cup fill with questionable vending machine coffee when Cate came in, fatigue marking her face. She was wearing tan slacks, a dark brown turtleneck. As usual, she wore very little makeup or jewelry, just a gold necklace and small teardrop earrings. As I watched her cross the room, she brushed her hair back from her face with one hand in a mannerism I had always found suggestive and alluring.

"Coffee?" I asked.

"If I drink another drop, I'll have to give up sleep for the rest of my life," Cate said, shaking her head.

"You been here all night?"

She nodded as she sat down heavily at an empty table near a window.

"How's he doing?"

"He'll survive. No permanent injuries, at least physically. He's asleep right now. Do you want to see him?"

I looked at her and shook my head as I sipped the coffee. A trace of disappointment flickered across her eyes.

"Has he said anything else to you about what happened?" I asked, changing the subject.

"I've asked, but he won't talk to me about it."

"Tell me about Sarita Ramirez."

"Kyle and Sarita live together, and I presume it's a longstanding relationship even though I'd never met her until two days ago."

"The next time you see her find out what she meant about knowing this would happen."

"She's supposed to be here soon. Why don't you talk to her?"

"I think it would be better if I stayed in the background. If I question her, she's bound to tell him. You make a living getting people to say things they don't want to, counselor. Get her to talk to you. Where are you staying?" I asked.

"There's a Holiday Inn a few blocks from here on Durango."

"I was kinda hoping you were staying at his place. Then maybe I could sneak a peek at his notes and see what's there."

"Sorry. Sarita didn't invite me, and I didn't ask." Cate leaned back in her chair and crossed her arms.

I stared at the coffee grounds in the bottom of my cup. "Have you told him you came to see me?"

As Cate turned her eyes toward me, there was something unreadable in them. "Quite honestly, Jo, you haven't been a topic of conversation. You lived your life, and we lived ours. Life went on. Is that what you want to know?"

Well, I asked for that one, I thought. Too bad she wasn't a fucking mute. We had never had any problems unless we talked.

"You recommend the Holiday Inn?" I asked after a few moments of awkward silence.

"It's comfortable enough, but I'm only going to be here a couple of days."

"Okay, I've probably stayed in worse places," I said, finishing my coffee and standing up. "See if you can lay your hands on a key to his place and have a copy made for me. Then before you head back to the Capital City, arrange to get this Sarita here with you sometime, so I can check out their apartment. After that, you can go on home."

"How long will you be here?"

"Hard to tell right now."

"I appreciate you coming, Jo. I wasn't sure you would," she said as she reached out and touched my arm.

Her touch surprised me. It was always hot and cold with her. Fifteen years earlier that touch had meant everything to me, but now it brought me too close to the past, and I stepped away. "Yeah, well, neither was I."

I found the Holiday Inn near Market Square and checked in, staying only long enough to drop my bags on the bed and buy a map of San Antonio. I spent the next three or four hours passing myself off as a family friend. Kyle's editor at the Light had no idea what story he was working on but let me look through his desk. The bottom drawer held scraps of paper with notes on them as well as a couple of filled notebooks. When no one was looking, I stuffed them into my jacket pockets.

The police were less cooperative. They weren't talking about the case period, other than to refer me to the public defender's office. Because the suspect was a juvenile, the little shit's name wasn't even available. And with the victim still alive, I doubted the case would have a very high priority. The public defender's office was closed by the time I got there, and I decided to give up for the evening and start again in the morning. I was lying on the bed watching the evening news when the phone next to me rang.

"Yeah," I answered.

"Jo?" It was Cate.

"You just get in?"

"Yes, and I have the key you wanted."

"What room are you in? I'll come and get it."

"Three-thirty-four."

"Be there in a minute."

I knocked on the door to Cate's room and stood where I could be seen through the security peephole. Cate opened the door and handed me a key that still had the tag from an instant key place on it.

"I'll need the address, too."

Picking up a complimentary ballpoint pen from the nightstand, Cate wrote the address on motel stationary. "It's not too far from here. I've only been there once, but I think I can remember how to get there if you want me to show you where it is."

"When will Sarita not be there?" I asked, ignoring her offer.

"The only time I could arrange for her to be at the hospital with me is Saturday morning. The doctor is planning to discharge Kyle from the hospital then, and she'll be there to drive him home. I'm returning to Austin as soon as he's released. How long will you need?"

"Forty minutes. Maybe an hour."

"That shouldn't be a problem. It takes forever to check out of a hospital, and I can stall if I have to about the billing."

"Give me a call here when she's at the hospital, and that will be that," I said as I reached for the doorknob.

"Have you had dinner yet?" Cate asked. "I was just going to go down to get something."

"I was considering room service when you called."

"I wouldn't mind some company. I hate eating alone."

"Sure." I shrugged.

I opened the door, and we were halfway out when the phone rang.

"Hello. Oh, hello. I was going to call you later," she said with a quick glance in my direction. "He's better today and should be out Saturday."

She rubbed her forehead and lowered her voice.

"I know when the banquet is, Susan," she said with a

hint of irritation in her voice, "and I'll be there if I can. Don't worry about picking me up. I'll drive myself."

She looked toward me again and gave a half smile.

"Can I call you back? I'm starving and was just on my way to get something."

A couple of uh-huhs later she hung up and rejoined me at the door.

The restaurant in the hotel was pleasant, and the waitress was extremely friendly. Cate ordered grilled trout after the waitress assured her it was absolutely fresh, practically dragged in from the river that very afternoon, while I ordered enchiladas and a Corona Light. Even though I had had the same meal about six hours earlier, it's my belief that you can never have enough of a good thing.

"I see your taste in food hasn't changed," Cate said as the waitress left to get our drinks.

"Kinda hate to give up a good thing once I've found it," I said, realizing how ironic that must have sounded to Cate.

There were a few empty tables in the dining room, but they filled quickly with traveling businessmen who immediately engrossed themselves in copies of the New York Times and the Wall Street Journal.

"You going back to the hospital tonight?" I asked.

"No. Kyle told me to get a good night's sleep on a real bed. After the last two nights in a recliner, I didn't argue with him too much."

"Who is Susan, or is that none of my business?" I asked.

Cate smiled. "It isn't, but she's my law partner."

"You doing corporate work now?"

"Mostly."

"I thought you loved that pacing back and forth in front of a jury thing."

"I did, but it didn't pay as well. Most of our clients are corporations with money to burn. I handle civil suits brought against them, and Susan does their tax law. I get into court occasionally, but we manage to settle most cases before they get in front of a jury."

The waitress returned and set drinks in front of us.

"You like it then?" I asked.

"It gets boring occasionally, but the money is good."

"What about the money in your trust?"

"It's still there. I'll turn it over to Kyle next year, I suppose."

"You were supposed to be living on it, Cate. That's why I set it up to begin with."

"Actually, I did use some of the trust money three or four years ago. Kyle and a friend of his from college wanted to go to Europe and do that same old thing all kids want to do. Essentially that was his graduation present from you."

"Did he enjoy himself?"

"Very much," Cate said as she squeezed lemon into her tea. "You've missed a lot by not being involved in his life."

"All I was going to do was drop in and out of his life. It didn't work with you and me, and it wouldn't have worked with him either. Mom kept me up on what he was doing."

"We used to go to the ranch quite a bit, you know. We attended your father's funeral a couple of years ago. Your mother said they hadn't been able to contact you."

"Red Cross didn't deliver the message to me until the day of the funeral. There wasn't anything I could do at that point," I said.

I was relieved when the waitress returned with our food. After she was assured that we didn't need anything else and thought she had done enough to earn an adequate tip, she moved on to another table. Mixing a forkful of enchilada with Spanish rice, I chewed the food slowly. I'd had better.

"How did you know I was back at the ranch?" I asked, washing down a mouthful of food with the cold beer.

"I called your mother," Cate said as she speared a bite-size piece of trout with her fork. "Wherever you were I thought you should know about Kyle. I was surprised when she told me you were back in Kerrville."

"I didn't know you were still in touch with my family."

"Just because things didn't work between you and me didn't mean I wanted to cut Kyle off from your family. What made you decide to move back?"

"Got tired of living out of a duffel bag, I guess." I shrugged. "After Dad died and Mom moved to be closer to my sister, I didn't want to see the ranch sold off."

"You bought it?"

"Seemed like a good idea at the time, and Mom won't have to worry financially."

Cate smiled at me. "Well, it's always been in your nature to be generous...at least with your money."

We ate quietly through most of the meal. Being with

Cate had once seemed like the most comfortable, natural thing in the world, but now we were reduced to inane chitchat.

I felt much better by the time I polished off the enchiladas, and Cate was beginning to look more relaxed, too. She had an interesting face. Never exactly beautiful, but at moments, she looked exquisite. It was her eyes. They made her face.

"I know it's a little late, and none of my business, but how have you been since we separated, Cate?" I asked.

"I have a good job, a comfortable home, a nice car, good friends, and a son every parent dreams of. I couldn't ask for much more."

"But you're still living alone."

"That doesn't mean I'm lonely," Cate said with a smile that suggested she hadn't been.

"Is that where Susan comes into the picture?"

"That really isn't any of your business."

"You're right. I was just wondering why you haven't sought another relationship. If not for yourself, then for Kyle. Two parents and all that Dr. Spock bullshit."

"Who's Lena?"

I laughed out loud. "You can't be serious! Lena is my housekeeper. Hell, Cate, I didn't have time for you. What makes you think I'd have time for more than a week or two with another woman. Guess I just figured you'd get lonely."

"I didn't feel the need for another permanent relationship, but I haven't been lonely. And I can't imagine you've been lonely very often either."

"Touché, counselor."

Cate laughed and I felt good when I heard her. Laughter lit up her eyes, and although she was older, her eyes were the same deep blue that drew me into them.

Chapter
Four

THE FIRST TIME I had seen Cathryn Hammond, I was
sitting in an Austin jail cell and had to admit that I didn't look
my best. If first impressions were important, I was certain I
had failed miserably. All I had wanted was a few laughs and a
couple of beers. My plane had landed at six-thirty, and by ten-
thirty, I was in jail charged with drunk and disorderly,
assault and battery, resisting arrest, and various other minor
charges. My ribs hurt, my knuckles hurt, and I hadn't even
had a chance to finish more than one dance. Being an
upstanding citizen, I had demanded an attorney. And what
did they send me? This girl who looked like she couldn't even
spell jurisprudence yet. By the time she arrived, I was already
pissed off about my homecoming. Standing over the stainless
steel sink in my cell, I splashed water on my face and tried to
catch a glimpse of myself in the reflection off the metal. I
couldn't tell if I needed stitches or not, but the bitch I fought
with had been wearing a big-ass ring that had torn open a
place under my left eye that felt like the Grand Canyon.

"Carlisle!" the jailer called.

I turned my head toward her. Her dark hair was pulled
back into a severe bun, and she reminded me of the
stereotypical jailhouse matron of Forties B-movie fame. Her
uniform obviously was general issue, and the shirt buttons
strained against her ample breasts.

"You sick?" she asked with no genuine concern in her
voice.

"No," I said.

"Well, your lawyer's here."

"It's about damn time," I said as I grabbed my jacket and
waited for her to open the cell door. She followed behind me,
giving instructions on where to turn and when to stop. We

finally stopped in front of a door marked Interview Room Four, and she pushed the door open, holding it until I entered the room.

"I'll be right outside in case you need me, ma'am," the jailer said.

I looked toward the table, and Cate stood up to greet her new client. Turning back toward the door, I pushed it open, coming face to face with the jailer.

"This is a joke, right?" I asked.

"You said you wanted a lawyer. You got one. Now go in, sit down, and shut up before you wind up back in the cellblock."

She shut the door and resumed her position outside.

"Ms. Carlisle," I heard the young woman say and turned to look at her, shaking my head as I went to a chair across the table from this novice. "I'm Cathryn Hammond, and I've been appointed to represent you," she said as I sat down.

"How long have you been out of law school?" I asked.

"Long enough for your purposes," she said matter-of-factly as she opened a folder in front of her. "You're charged with drunk and disorderly, assault and battery, destruction of private property, and resisting arrest."

"Yeah, that about sums it up. Got any suggestions?"

"Why don't you tell me your version of what happened, and we can go from there." She flipped open a legal pad and looked at me.

"I've been out of the country for a few months. I flew in late this afternoon planning to visit my folks down near Kerrville. But I decided to check out the club action here before I drove home, so I rented a car and found a cozy little country-western bar. I was just having a beer and checking out the local ladies when this big dyke came up to me and accused me of ogling her woman. Next thing I know the fists are flying."

"And you couldn't have ignored her, I suppose?" Cate asked with the hint of a smile that made me feel like she understood.

"Sure I could've and I planned to, right up to when she dumped a drink over my head. I figured she wasn't going to leave it alone, so I smacked her."

"You hit her first then."

"Well, I wasn't going to sit there with beer dripping off

of me and wait for her next move. She wanted trouble, and I obliged."

"Were you drunk?"

"I was in the midst of my first beer when the trouble started. It's probable that given more time, I would've gotten drunk. But, no, I wasn't."

"But the other woman was drunk?"

"As a skunk."

"According to witness statements, you hit her several times. If she was that drunk, wouldn't one blow have been sufficient?"

I leaned forward and rested my arms on the table and smiled at Cate. "Probably, but I've been suppressing a lot of pent-up hostility lately. Besides, as you may have noticed, she still managed to get in a hit or two herself."

"Has anyone looked at that yet?"

"Do you think I'll need stitches?" I asked, gingerly fingering my cheek.

"Probably just a butterfly bandage. I'll make sure someone looks at it before I leave."

"To tell you the truth, I don't know why I was even arrested." Holding up one finger at a time, I recounted the situation as I saw it. "She assaulted me. I defended myself. I wasn't drunk. I'm willing to pay my share of damages to the owners. What's the problem?"

"I think most of this can be handled without going to court, but there is the resisting arrest."

"I didn't think I should be arrested, and those nice officers and I had a little...discussion about it."

Cate smiled again and asked, "You seem to have a pretty quick temper. What exactly is it that you do for a living, Ms. Carlisle?"

"Photojournalist."

"Where were you?"

"Middle East," I said.

"I would think you saw enough fighting there without bringing it home with you."

"I had to put up with plenty of bullshit while I was there. I sure as hell didn't need to put up with it at home. How soon can I get out of here?"

"Probably in the morning. But you'll have to post bail and return for trial."

"I don't have time for a trial, sweetheart. Just fix it and

I'll pay whatever the fine is. I have another assignment at the beginning of the month."

"I'll do what I can, but I can't make any promises," Cate said as she closed her pad and placed it in her briefcase. Raising her eyes to mine and holding my gaze, she said, "If this does go to trial, however, I'd advise you to work on curbing that smart-ass butch mouth of yours, and let me do the talking."

"I'll consider it." I smiled.

Chapter
Five

AS I BACKED the Blazer out of the hotel parking lot early the next morning, I glanced at a piece of paper in my hand before turning onto the access road.

My last call the night before had been to Wendell Pauli, a retired San Antonio vice detective. I had known Pauli since my rookie reporter days in San Antonio, and although I wasn't sure how much help a vice cop would be, he might be able to steer me in the right direction. Pauli's wife had died a couple of years earlier, and he claimed his kids had disowned him long before that. He sounded sober on the phone, but after all the years that had passed, I wasn't sure what to expect.

The directions to his house were precise and contained only four or five turnoffs. It wasn't a great neighborhood now, but once upon a time it had obviously been at least upper middle class. Like all older neighborhoods, however, the whole area had eased, not so gracefully, into an economic decline. Large trees lined Pauli's street and had been there long enough to buckle the sidewalks in front of a few places. Most of the houses were split-level ranch-style homes, and a number of them appeared to be vacant. The newest part of each house seemed to be burglar bars. By the time I located the address Pauli had given me, I saw that it was the only house without burglar bars, almost an invitation to burglars. A low well-trimmed hedge ran from the sidewalk to the house, and there was a slight embankment broken by a couple of cement steps.

As I rang the doorbell and waited, I noticed there was a conspicuous absence of children or children's toys in the yards of the houses along the street and guessed that most of the inhabitants were well beyond their childbearing years.

When Pauli finally opened the front door, I almost asked if I had the right house. There was absolutely no resemblance to the Wendell Pauli in my memory bank. His head was a hairless cueball with a single, gray-black eyebrow separating his forehead from the rest of his face. He weighed at least a hundred pounds more than I remembered, and evidence of too many big meals and too many beers hung over the waistband of his pants. His black T-shirt, emblazoned with "I Love My Attitude Problem," looked two sizes too small, and a well-chewed cigar was clinched tightly between his teeth.

He pushed the front screen door open and motioned me inside without saying a word. I followed him down a dark hallway and into a small room that had been converted into an office. As he plopped down in a well-worn leather chair behind a scarred wooden desk, I could see that he either hadn't been up long enough to shave or had decided it wasn't a top priority today.

"You ain't changed much, Carlisle," he rumbled in a voice much deeper than I remembered, probably the result of abusing his vocal chords and lungs for decades with tobacco.

"Can't say the same for you, Pauli. I thought I had the wrong house for a minute."

"Have any trouble findin' the place?" he asked, ignoring my remark.

"No. You give excellent directions," I said as I looked around the office. Dozens of city and state citations hung on the walls, but it lacked the usual personal pictures you'd expect to see. Maybe he was telling the truth about his family, and there was no love lost among them.

"Didn't know you had a kid."

"My ex and I adopted him so I guess I'm a step-something. I haven't seen either one of them in about fifteen years."

"But now she expects you to bail the kid out."

"She doesn't expect it, but she asked if there was anything I could do," I said. I knew that if there had been another human being on the planet Cate thought could help she wouldn't have contacted me. "That's why I'm here," I continued.

"What do you expect me to do for you?"

I took a few minutes to explain what I had already

learned, which admittedly wasn't much.

"I might be able to do somethin' about findin' out the shooter's name, and the Ivy Leaguers he runs with," Pauli said. He got up and pulled open a file drawer and thumbed through a drawerful of manila folders. "I brought copies of all my files with me when I retired," he said as he continued looking.

"You still have informants?"

"Every now and then I drop in on a few of 'em just for fun. If I didn't keep my hand in, even a little bit, I'd probably go off the deep end."

He pulled five or six folders from the drawer and pushed it shut with his hip before sitting down again.

"Tell you what, Carlisle. Let's take a run down to the precinct where they're holdin' the shooter and see if I can pick up the name. If that don't work, I'll go over to the public defender's office and pass myself off as active duty. Those damn yuppies at the PD's office never know what to do when they're confronted. If you're real lucky, they'll have a rookie assigned to the case. So leave that part to me."

"Then what?"

"You say you ain't talked to your kid yet?"

"I don't want him to know his mother asked me for help," I said. "He already hates my guts. No sense in turning him against her as well."

"Sounds like me and my family." Pauli grunted. "Okay, then I'll take that one, too."

"What do you have in mind?"

"I'll drop by his room and do a little interrogatin'. He might inadvertantly let somethin' useful slip about this big story he's workin' on. But honestly, Jo, illegals..." He shook his head.

"I know. Illegals aren't a big story. It's got to be something deeper than that, Pauli. Maybe it just started with illegals and then got off into something else."

"Got any brilliant thoughts on that one?"

"Not yet, but tomorrow morning I'm searching his apartment."

Pauli smiled. "I don't suppose you got permission to do that."

"My ex gave me the key. That good enough?"

"Nope. It ain't her apartment."

"I'm just looking around. I won't take anything."

"Let me know if you need any help. I got one of those spy camera gizmos if you need it. Don't have any film for the damn thing though."

"I'll get some just in case, but there might not be anything to find."

I stood up and held my hand out. "I appreciate this, Pauli. Let me know how much time you spend on this, and I'll reimburse you."

He slapped my hand. "I ain't no private dick, woman. Just the fun will be payment enough. You know how much I like roustin' folks." He laughed.

He picked up the folders and handed them to me. "Hang onto these while I get into somethin' a little more official-lookin'. You can wait in the car while I see what I can find out. Won't take long."

Twenty minutes later, Pauli came into the living room wearing a blue two-piece suit over a white shirt and adjusting a red and white striped tie. From the look of the suit, I doubted he could button it. He had shaved the stubble from his face and rubbed at it absently. Following him out a back door and into a two-car garage, we climbed into an old, tan Chrysler Belvedere.

With the touch of a button clipped on the visor, the garage door ground open. Pauli threw the car in reverse and backed down the drive onto the street. Cursing other drivers as incompetent morons, he broke every traffic law I was familiar with on the ride to the police precinct. I was forced to close my eyes more than once, fighting the impulse to tighten my seatbelt, and breathed a sigh of relief when he finally whipped the vehicle into the parking lot of the police station and slammed on the brakes. For a man his size, he was amazingly nimble as he exited the car and trotted toward the entrance to the building, stopping long enough to speak to a couple of officers he passed on the sidewalk. They slapped shoulders and spoke briefly before he continued into the building.

With nothing else to do while I waited, I glanced through the folders he had given me. What lay in front of me were some of the pathetic dregs of San Antonio underlife. Most were petty criminals no one would want to run into in a dark alley. By the time I finished reading the last folder, Pauli was pulling open the driver's door. He wedged himself behind the wheel and turned the key in the ignition and winked.

"Piece a cake," he said with a smile. "The shooter is one Fernando Acevedo, age eleven years and seven months. Just under the limit."

"What limit?"

"Once a kid turns twelve the state can declare him an adult in serious cases. Under that and juvenile detention is practically a done deal. Also got an address and mama's name. Wanna check out the homeboy's neighborhood and shake a few trees to see if anything falls out?"

"I guess so."

"I can do it alone if you want."

"Is that where the shooting took place?"

"Naw. The kid must have used public transportation, or someone dropped him off. They recovered the weapon, but surprise, surprise, no serial number. A real hunk of junk."

"I feel dumb asking this, Pauli, but where did the shooting happen?"

"Parkin' lot of the Light. Stupid little fuck wouldn't have been caught if he hadn't hung around a little too long."

Pauli backed out of the parking space and drove like a man possessed until we were within a few blocks of Acevedo's address. The area wasn't just economically deprived; the economy had never reached this section of town. For a fleeting moment it crossed my mind that if I were a kid living there, I might take a hundred bucks to shoot someone, too. Drunks from the night before were still curled up in doorways and down alleys. There were plenty of children around, but none of them looked like they were on their way to school even though it was a school day. Everything about the buildings and street was oppressive. I'd seen better conditions in Fourth World countries. For a booming metropolis—the ninth largest city in the United States—prosperity obviously wasn't evenly distributed, and I wondered how many of the people living here were legal. Pauli interrupted my thoughts.

"Say, ain't one of them folders on a guy named Mercado?"

"I think so," I said, looking quickly through the folders again. "Yeah, David Mercado. Why?"

"'Cause there the hunk of shit is," Pauli said, pointing to a shaggy-headed man who appeared to be in his late thirties. He was shuffling down the sidewalk wearing jeans with holes at the knees and in the back pockets. I had seen kids shell out big bucks for similar attire, but in Mercado's case, the holes were not a fashion statement.

Pauli swung the car across the street next to the man and rolled the window down.

"Hey, Mercado!"

The man looked surprised, as if he hadn't seen the car pull over. A scraggly beard covered the lower part of his face, and he blinked incessantly as he looked at us. Pauli opened his door and stepped from the car. As I got out, Pauli motioned for Mercado to join us near the rear of the Belvedere. Mercado looked around to see who else was on the street before moving. He jammed his hands into the pockets of his dirty jeans and shifted his weight to one foot.

"I heard you was retired, Pauli," he said in a hoarse voice.

"Can't believe everything you hear, Davey."

"Who's the bitch?" Mercado asked, nodding toward me.

"New partner. I need some information about a case."

"I need to get laid. So what?"

"Looks more like you need a fix to me."

"Hey, I'm clean now, man," Mercado said as he pulled a hand from his pocket and ran it under his nose.

Pauli chuckled. "Yeah, right. You know a kid named Fernando Acevedo?"

"Nando?"

"Yeah. He lives a couple of blocks from here."

"He got a real fine-lookin' mama," Mercado said as he closed one eye against the sun and squinted at us.

"He a hitter?"

"Nando's a punk."

"He a banger?"

"Don't know." Mercado shrugged. "Maybe."

"If he was, which boys would be his?"

Mercado laughed derisively. "You goin' senile or somethin', ol' man? You know whose turf this is."

"Conquistadors, right?"

A nod.

"Anybody more unusual than normal been hangin' around lately? Anybody from out of the area kickin' up a little business with the Conquistadors?"

"Ain't seen nobody."

"Conquistadors involved with bringin' in illegals?"

"Shit, Pauli, they be mostly illegals theyselves. Bring

more in and all they gonna do is make their own gang. Conquistadors don't need no fuckin' competition."

"Who's in charge now?"

"I heard Escobar."

"Freddie?"

Another nod.

"Still holdin' court in the same place?"

A shrug.

Pauli pulled his wallet out and waved a twenty at Mercado. It was the first time he looked awake since Pauli stopped him.

"Take this, Davey," Pauli said as he pulled a pen from his pocket and wrote on the bill. "You see anyone meetin' with the Conquistadors who looks like they don't belong here, call that number and leave a message. You get somethin' and I'll have a few more Jacksons for you."

Mercado stuffed the bill into his pocket and continued down the street.

"Think he'll call?" I asked.

"Who knows? Depends on how strung out he gets. Escobar screwed him over a few years ago. He might want to get even."

"What are you hunting for anyway, Pauli?" I asked as we returned to the car.

"Well, sometimes outsiders who want to contract out a hit contact these morons down here to do it. It's cheaper than bringing in a pro from out of town. Of course, the results ain't as reliable, but it usually works pretty good. If your kid tripped onto something else besides your basic illegal angle, whoever is involved might have hired one of these kiddies to do the job to keep the focus on illegals rather than draw attention to themselves."

"Sounds a little convoluted."

"Crime gets that way sometimes," Pauli said as he folded himself back into the vehicle.

We cruised the rest of the neighborhood before Pauli returned to his house to drop me off. He was going to the hospital to interview Kyle and then planned to convince some old pal on the force to give him access to the computer to check a few things. I gave him Sarita Ramirez's name and asked him to check her out as well. Pauli agreed to pick me up the following morning to search Kyle's apartment.

When I got back to my room at the hotel, I placed an

order with room service and started dialing numbers again.
I renewed a few old acquaintances, but otherwise the calls
were fruitless. Then I remembered the notebooks and scraps
of paper I had taken from Kyle's desk at the Light and found
them still stuffed in my jacket pockets. While I waited for
my food, I spread the scraps of paper out on the bed and
began going through them one at a time. Most were phone
numbers and initials, and I added them to my list of phone
calls just to see if anyone interesting answered. There had
been two notebooks in Kyle's desk. One of them was over a
year old, but the second one was at least dated the current
year, and I started with it. I was about a fourth of the way
through when there was a knock at my door. Grabbing my
wallet, I went to the door, but when I opened it, it wasn't my
dinner.

"Did you send that fat cretin to the hospital today,
Joanna?" Cate asked as she barged into my room.

"Pauli?"

"Yes."

"I didn't send him, but he said he was going to ask Kyle
a few questions. Why?"

"He practically accused Kyle of shooting himself!"

"Calm down, Cate. He's just trying to get some
information."

"Well, he's not very subtle about it."

"Have you ever met a subtle cop? The kid won't tell you
what he's working on. His girlfriend won't say, and his
editor doesn't know shit. If you want my help, then we have
to get beyond subtle."

"He insinuated that Kyle was involved in something
illegal himself and that was why he was shot."

"I didn't tell him to do that, Cate. But for all I know the
kid might be involved in something illegal."

"That's absurd! And will you stop calling him 'the kid'!
He's your son, for God's sake!" She began pacing around the
room with her arms crossed in front of her. She came to a
halt in front of me, and when she looked at me, her eyes still
had a fire in them.

"Isn't it possible that you don't know him as well as you
think you do?" I asked.

"I know he wouldn't be involved in anything illegal."

"Well, apparently you didn't know he was shacked up
with the lovely senorita Sarita. What else don't you know?"

She swung her hand to slap me, but I caught her wrist before she could make contact.

"I should never have brought you into this. We were better off pretending you didn't exist," she seethed.

If she had hit me, it couldn't have hurt any more than her words had.

"Well, it's not too late, sweetheart," I shot back as I released her arm. "Say the word and I can be checked out of this dump in five minutes. If you want me to keep checking, I will. Then you can head on back to Susan and your clients, and let me do what I do."

Another knock at the door interrupted our conversation.

"Come in!"

A young Hispanic man opened the door and brought a tray into the room. He set it on the nightstand and took the tip I offered him, closing the door as he left. As soon as he was gone, I turned back toward Cate, who was still upset and fighting to regain control of herself.

"What's it going to be, Cate?"

"If you stay, will you at least let me know what's going on?"

"As long as you remember that I'll tell you if I discover anything bad as well."

"I know," Cate said, softening her tone slightly. "But you won't find anything bad."

"I hope you're right. Want half a sandwich?"

The argument had caused me to lose my appetite, and I began dialing more phone numbers as Cate picked at my sandwich. After nearly half an hour, I came to the conclusion that there were way too many takeout joints in San Antonio. I rested against the headboard and closed my eyes tightly.

"Tired?" Cate asked.

"I hate goddamn telephones. You can't look the speaker in the eyes and tell whether they're lying to you or not."

"They don't bother me. Let me call for a while. What am I looking for?"

"I don't have the slightest idea. I found these numbers in the kid's...I mean Kyle's desk at the paper and borrowed them. I was hoping one of them would be a person rather than a business or that there would just be something unusual about one of them."

"You mean something like Mafia Southwest, Inc.?" she said with a grin.

"At least that would be useful. Would you mind if I grabbed a quick shower? Pauli and I went to a couple of places today that reeked of garbage."

"Be my guest," she said as she picked up the receiver and looked at the numbers.

I was back in less than ten minutes. Cate was sitting on the edge of the bed and had a motel notepad and pen on the nightstand next to the phone. I had slipped into old jeans and a T-shirt and was barefoot. The carpet wasn't plush but felt good under my feet. Cate was wearing a pair of reading glasses that sat halfway down her nose. She glanced at me over the top of them as I came back into the room and tossed my dirty clothes into a corner. Steam from the bathroom followed me as I grabbed a hairbrush from the dresser and made a couple of quick swipes through my short graying brown hair before sitting down in a chair across from her. About half the sandwich was still on the plate and I took a bite and waited.

"Anything?" I asked with my mouth half full as she finally hung up the phone.

"Spoke to Sarita's mother in Dallas. This is the number in case you need it," she said, handing me a slip of paper. "So far the others are an assortment of businesses." She picked up another scrap of paper and looked at it. She dialed and then pulled her glasses off and let them dangle in her hand as the phone rang. From her reaction I assumed the phone was answered by a machine. She listened and then hung up. "That might be something, Jo. It was the San Antonio office of the Immigration and Naturalization Service."

"Could have been for background information on anything though."

"Were you planning to call all of these numbers tonight?" she asked, looking at the list. "I always thought your work was exciting, but this is more boring than what I do."

"Give your ear a rest. What time is the girlfriend supposed to be at the hospital in the morning?"

"Around nine. I'll call you here."

"Pauli's going to go with me, but I promise we won't disturb anything."

"Kyle has a computer. Whatever you're looking for might be on a CD."

"Oh, great," I muttered.

"You know how to use a computer, don't you?"

"Never felt the need to learn, but Pauli might."

Cate looked at her wristwatch. "I better go. I have a few calls to make myself. Unfortunately work didn't stop just because I was gone."

"Can't your law partner handle them?"

"Probably, but you know what they say about doing things yourself so you know they're done correctly." She got up and crossed to the door.

"Give Susan my regards," I said.

"Not likely," she said over her shoulder as she left my room.

I shook my head and smiled to myself. I had missed the little barbs we used to throw at each other. We had easily slipped back into them as if we had never been apart.

Chapter
Six

PAULI SHOWED UP earlier than I expected the next morning. I had a T-shirt halfway over my head when I opened the door. Pauli smiled, revealing tobacco-stained teeth, and held up two large cups of 7-11 coffee. A chewed-up stub of a cigar was clinched between his teeth, and I wondered if he slept with the damn thing in his mouth. He kicked the door closed with his foot as he entered the room.

"If I'd known you was sleepin' in, I would've called first," he said, handing me a Styrofoam cup.

"What time is it?"

"About seven. What time you supposed to perform your amateur sleuthin'?"

"The girlfriend isn't gonna be at the hospital until around nine. My ex will call when she arrives."

"That the spitfire I met yesterday?" he asked as he sipped from his cup.

"The way she tells it, you did everything but use a rubber hose on the kid."

"Tough little bastard. Wouldn't tell me shit even when I told him I knew the gist of his story. Gave me that First Amendment bullshit about confidentiality of sources and spit out a bunch of court cases I never heard of."

"His mother's a lawyer."

"Decent-lookin' woman."

I grunted and wandered into the bathroom to wash my face. Over coffee I recounted the phone calls from the day before, including the one to the INS.

"Reckon he's workin' on somethin' that might interest the Feds?" Pauli asked.

"Could've been for background information. For all I know those numbers are a year or more old."

"By the way, I ran the girlfriend's name through the police computer. She's clean, but a couple of her family members could use a sponge bath."

"How's that?"

"Mostly petty juvenile stuff, but she's got a brother who did a stint for some gang-related deal."

"In San Antonio?"

"Dallas. Probably just wanted to join up and got recruited in high school. He's out now and a straight shooter as far as I can tell."

"Maybe Kyle was using him as a source on gang activities."

Pauli shrugged and chewed on his cigar.

"You ever light that thing?" I asked.

He shook his head. "Smokin's bad for you."

We killed nearly two hours before the phone finally rang. I grabbed it before the first ring died away.

"She's here, Jo," Cate answered.

"Okay. Have a safe trip home," I said looking at Pauli.

He signaled to me with his hand. "Tell her to call the kid's place when they leave the hospital, so we can clear out. Let it ring two times and then hang up so we'll know it's her."

I relayed the message, and Cate agreed to call from her cell phone.

Within ten minutes we were at the building in Olmos Park where Kyle and Sarita shared an apartment. The area looked deserted as Pauli drove around the block. There was a back alley and a fire escape from each floor. In case we didn't make it out in time, Pauli wanted an alternative route out of the building. We parked across the street from the apartment building and walked in like a couple of regular tenants, taking the elevator to the fourth floor. I pushed my duplicate key into the lock, and we entered the living room.

The apartment was light and clean. Apparently Sarita Ramirez was a decent housekeeper. The living room was decorated in early discount store, but tastefully done. There were a few pictures hanging on the walls, mostly cheap prints probably bought along the River Walk from street artists, and cinder blocks and boards for bookshelves. While I looked around, Pauli had already explored the remainder of the apartment. It had two bedrooms with one converted into an office that wasn't as neat as the rest of the apartment.

Reporters took notes on whatever they could grab, and their general filing system was wherever they set it down later. I had hated it when Cate cleaned up my work area, driving myself crazy looking for addresses and phone numbers that Cate would neatly file under miscellaneous. More often than not, unless I knew where it was lying on my desk, I didn't know whose address or number it was. Pauli sat down at the desk with the computer in front of him.

"You check the drawers, and I'll see what's up with the computer," he said.

I pulled the drawers from the desk one at a time and went through them. In the bottom drawer were more notebooks. I fanned through them checking the dates, looking for anything Kyle had scribbled down in the last three or four months. Pauli turned on the computer and stuck a CD in the drive. Most of them contained parts of stories, but none were related to illegals. I found a couple of recent notebooks and wasn't happy to see that Kyle had developed his own version of shorthand. Mostly numbers and initials. But there were a couple of plain English notations that caught my interest.

"You bring the camera?" I asked Pauli as he scrolled through files on the CDs. Without stopping what he was doing, he reached into his jacket pocket and tossed me a little camera that looked like a prize from a Cracker Jack box.

Loading it with film, I snapped several pages, hoping the piece of junk in my hand worked.

"Ah-ha!" I heard Pauli say.

"Find something?"

"Found a CD that's protected. Kid's got about twenty of 'em here, and this is the only one that's protected."

"Can you copy it?"

"What good would that do? I don't know his password. If we had more time I know a guy who could probably get past it."

"Well, we don't have more time, and if it's got what we need on it, he'll probably check it pretty quick so we can't take it."

"Hell, could just be pornographic fantasies that he doesn't want his girlfriend to see." Pauli shrugged.

We continued looking for over an hour before the phone rang. When it rang a second time and stopped, we quickly finished what we were doing and left the apartment.

Sitting in Pauli's car, we watched Sarita pull a silver Nissan Sentra into a parking space in front of the apartment building half an hour later and open the trunk to remove a small bag. She was well dressed in a calf-length denim skirt, boots, and an embroidered blouse. A silver concho belt encircled her slim waist, and long black hair cascaded over her shoulders and down her back. She reminded me of Selma Hayak and it didn't take much deductive reasoning to see why Kyle had been attracted her. As Kyle slowly pulled himself out of the passenger seat, Sarita went to his side of the car, and I got my first glimpse of his face as he turned. He had grown into an extraordinarily handsome young man. His Hispanic heritage was obvious with thick black hair framing his olive complexion.

The last time I had seen him he had been wearing jeans and boots and was sitting on a horse at the ranch. He couldn't have been more than ten or eleven then, oblivious to the problems swirling around him, problems he might never understand.

It had been my last trip to the ranch with Cate and Kyle. I knew we didn't have a perfect relationship but hadn't realized how much trouble we were in. Who the hell was I kidding? I knew we were in serious trouble and had chosen to overlook it, hoping, like Herbert Hoover at the beginning of the Great Depression, that everything would work itself out on its own. And like Hoover, I had been wrong.

We hadn't been to the ranch in over a year and decided to drop in the day before I left on my next assignment. Cate and I had already had an argument before we arrived but tried to fake our way through the visit. I didn't know how much my mother had noticed, but my father had been annoyingly perceptive. An hour or so before we returned to Austin, he asked me to help him with something in the barn. Although we both knew he had never needed my help for anything, I went along anyway. He smacked me across the face as soon as we reached the barn.

"What the hell was that for?" I asked, feeling to see if my mouth was bleeding.

"I was hoping that would knock some sense into that thick head of yours. I've never butted into your personal life, Jo. You've always done everything your own way no matter what the consequences might be. But I'm telling you straight up that if you don't get your shit together you're going to lose Cate and Kyle."

"We'll work it out."

"How're you planning to do that when you're always halfway around the goddamn world? Mental telepathy? This is gonna be your third overseas assignment just this year!"

"After this assignment I'm taking some time off. Then I'll be home for more than a few days."

"You ain't got a home. You rent an apartment, for Christ's sake."

"Cate's looking for a house. Next time I'm home..."

But there never was a next time.

Chapter
Seven

MY COURTSHIP OF Cate Hammond had begun not long after she had magically gotten me out of jail. Although she had initially rejected the idea, the more she resisted the more I wanted to be with her. It had been a long time since I'd had to work that hard to be with a woman, but my whole life had been built around accepting challenges and taking risks.

My persistence finally paid off, and Cate agreed to have dinner with me. After dinner, we went to a women's bar to see what the local scene had to offer and decided to stick around a while for a drink. I had missed dancing, but it wasn't the dancing I was interested in. It was the chance to find out what she would feel like in my arms. She was a perfect fit. Sooner than I would have liked, she told me she had to be in court early the next morning, and I drove her home.

"Thanks, Jo," she said as we reached her door. "It was an interesting evening, and I haven't been out in a while."

"I can't believe you aren't asked out all the time," I said.

"I didn't say I wasn't asked out. I said I hadn't been out."

"I guess you must have a pretty heavy schedule at the defender's office."

"Usually."

What had been comfortable quickly became uncomfortable. I was thirty-two, but she made me feel eighteen and awkward again. I had been with my share of women overseas, but looking back on those encounters, I realized that those women all understood what was expected at the end of an evening and were prepared for it without lengthy or meaningful conversation. This was a different situation, and I wasn't sure how to handle it.

"I'd like to see you again, Cate."

"I don't know, Jo. I've got a pretty full week ahead."

"You can't work every night."

"If I want to be prepared for court I have to. Everything can't be done at the office."

"What about the weekend? Don't you take a break then?"

"Sometimes on Sunday."

Reaching out and placing my hand on her arm, I said, "Then let me have Sunday."

Cate looked at my hand on her arm and smiled. I stepped closer to her and looked into those deep blue eyes as I leaned down and kissed her. As I kissed her more deeply a second time, her lips parted, and she made no effort to resist my advances. When our lips finally parted, she smiled at me. I wanted her and she knew it.

"Cate..."

"Sunday," she said.

When Sunday finally arrived, an eternity later, Cate fixed breakfast in the morning, and we made love the rest of the day. From Sunday until the day I boarded my plane a week later, we were together. In the evenings, we prepared dinner together, and I helped her prepare cases. She practiced opening and closing statements on me. I loved talking to her and simple things pleased her. We talked about world events, cussed and discussed politics, and she was, frankly, the first woman I had been with in a long time who knew more than single-syllable words.

The day I left, she drove me to the airport and waited with me at the gate. The waiting area of one airport looks pretty much the same in every airport, but I had never noticed how crowded they were before. The excruciatingly uncomfortable plastic seats were bolted to the floor and had obviously been designed by sadistic dwarves. There were so many people sitting and milling around that it was difficult to carry on a conversation. Little kids played tag to kill time and, left unattended by their parents, jumped over our legs.

"I wish I didn't have to go," I said.

"We knew you'd be leaving, Jo. It's what you do." She smiled.

"It doesn't seem fair to you, asking you to wait."

"I've got plenty to keep me busy here. Thanks for helping me with my cases."

"I had an ulterior motive." I grinned. "The faster you

got finished with what you were doing, the faster I could get you into bed."

When my flight number was called, I stood up and took Cate's hand.

"I'll be back in a month or two. I'll call to let you know."

Cate smiled and hugged me. "I'll save Sunday for you."

That was how we spent our time for almost a year — me going away and returning after long absences, and Cate always giving me Sunday no matter what day of the week it really was.

I hadn't been happy about my next assignment when I returned to Austin that Christmas. It had been nearly three months since I had been home, and as the plane descended, I looked down and saw trees everywhere around the city. It was unusually warm for mid-December, according to the pilot, and he hoped everyone had enjoyed the flight.

I waited in my seat until nearly everyone else had deplaned to avoid injuring anyone with my duffel bag and camera case. Nodding to the stewardess, I started down the walkway and into the terminal. Cate was nowhere in sight, and I hoped she had gotten my telegram. Halfway down the concourse leading to the street, I finally saw her coming toward me and jogged the best I could with my bags, dropping everything to sweep her into my arms.

"I'm sorry I'm late," Cate said breathlessly. "Court adjourned late and traffic is terrible."

"It doesn't matter. You look great," I said, unable to restrain a smile.

Cate picked up my camera case and took my arm. Piling everything into the back seat of her car, we headed away from the airport.

"How long will you be home?" Cate asked as she checked for oncoming traffic at the airport exit.

"Through New Year's. Got any holiday plans?"

"A few." Cate smiled.

When we reached Cate's apartment, I dropped my bags on the bedroom floor, took Cate in my arms, and fell onto the bed. I wanted and needed to catch up on three months' worth of kisses and lovemaking in the eighteen days we had. We stopped to come up for air a few minutes later, but I couldn't let her go.

"Jo, we need to talk," Cate said as I nibbled at her neck.

"Sounds serious."

"Not really. It's just something I've been thinking about for a long time, and I'd already set the gears in motion before I met you ."

"Oh, this really sounds mysterious." I smiled.

"About a year ago, I began the paperwork to adopt a child. Yesterday, the agency I'm using called and said they have a two-year-old boy available and are having a difficult time placing him because of some health problems. They want to know if I would be interested."

"What kinds of health problems?"

"His mother is an alcoholic and didn't spend much time taking care of him. He's malnourished and underweight and," she paused.

"And what?"

"He has a cleft palate that has never been repaired. That's why he's malnourished."

"I see," I said.

"Surgery can correct his palate, but it will be a lengthy process. The state removed him from his home and will pay for most of the medical expenses."

"What else do you know about his parents?"

"I know his mother is Hispanic, but the agency knows virtually nothing about his father except that he's Caucasian."

"That's a lot of baggage for a kid to carry around, Cate."

"But a good home now while he's still so young can give him the chance to live a good life."

Cate had hit the ball into my court, and I wasn't sure how to return it. I loved Cate, but children hadn't been in my immediate, or even distant, plans.

"I've never heard you mention wanting to becoming a mother before."

"I've been thinking about it for a few years. Adoption seemed the only logical option, considering my lifestyle."

"Then I guess the choice is yours, sweetheart." I shrugged.

"It involves you, too, Jo. Having a child in the house will change a lot of things."

I wasn't sure what Cate expected me to say. I stood up and looked down at her. "You know I'd do anything in the world for you, baby, but I've never even considered being a parent. I wish you'd mentioned this a little sooner."

"Would it have made a difference?" She frowned slightly, her eyes betraying her disappointment to my reaction.

"It might have. My job isn't exactly nine to five, and you'll be the one stuck at home with a kid. I've seen the workload you bring home at night, remember?"

"Actually, I've put out some feelers to enter private practice, which would allow me more free time in the evenings and on weekends."

"Sounds like you've been planning this for quite a while. I'm just not sure where I fit into this plan."

Cate stood next to me and put her arm around me. "I love you, Jo. I know you weren't expecting this, but I've always wanted a family. I was hoping you'd be as excited about it as I am."

I hugged Cate and held her tightly. "I love you, too, baby," I said, even though I had to rate my excitement level at less than zero.

I loved Cate but had to admit that I wasn't much of a parent. Kyle Eric Hammond had faced life's obstacles since his birth. Now, at twenty-seven, he was still finding the world a difficult place to live in.

Chapter
Eight

I WAS BROUGHT back to reality by Pauli whipping into a parking slot of the Holiday Inn. As I got out of his Chrysler, I saw Cate standing next to her metallic blue Cadillac Seville. Handing Pauli the key card to my room, I went toward her.

"Did you find anything?" she asked.

"Not much. I have to develop some film and see if I can figure out his hieroglyphics. There was one CD that might have had something on it, but it was protected, and we were hesitant to take it."

Cate handed me a business card with her name embossed on the front.

"Bradley and Hammond," I read aloud. "Very elegant."

"My home number is on the back along with the private number to my office and my cell phone number."

"How come you let Susan get top billing?" I smiled.

"Alphabetical order. And since she invited me to join her firm, I'm really the junior partner."

"I'll let you know if anything exciting happens. Otherwise, don't hold your breath."

"Let me have your cell number in case I need to contact you," Cate said as she fished a pen from her purse.

"Never use 'em."

She looked at me in disbelief. "You're not kidding, are you?"

"Nope. I had to use one for a couple of years while I was on assignments in the States, but I never remembered to charge the fuckin' thing or wasn't close enough to a tower to pick up reception. Besides, now that I'm retired, there isn't anyone I either want or need to talk to."

Cate nodded and got back into her car. I watched as she drove out of the parking lot before joining Pauli in my room.

Pauli and I spent the remainder of the morning and early afternoon trying to figure out what Kyle had written, without having much luck, and were both frustrated by the time we decided to give up.

"This James Bond shit is gettin' you nowhere," Pauli said. "You need someone on the inside to get close to the kid."

"You mean at the newspaper?"

"Yeah. At least to find out what the fuck this story is about besides illegals."

"I might know someone....if I can talk her into it."

"Who's that?" Pauli asked, stretching his huge frame.

"Stevie Leonard," I said.

"I thought she dropped off the radar screen after she got shot up in Mexico."

"She did. Last I heard she was living in a cabin somewhere along the Guadalupe."

"Weren't you two an item once upon a time?"

"Yeah." I frowned. "Once upon a time."

Stevie Leonard had been a moderately experienced photojournalist when she accompanied me to cover the Indian revolt in the Chiapas area of Mexico in 1994. We had been on two other assignments together prior to Chiapas and had found enough attractive about each other to entertain ourselves during our downtime. The situation in Chiapas had escalated faster than anyone anticipated, leaving us vulnerable. The Mexican government and army regulars hadn't wasted much of their time attempting to peacefully quell the revolt.

It had been a relatively peaceful afternoon when the quiet was shattered by the sound of sporadic gunfire and screaming. Reacting instinctively, we both grabbed our cameras and ran toward the action. Stevie was almost fifteen years younger and an exercise addict in good physical condition. When I made it over the top of a small rise close to the sounds of the gunfire, a few seconds behind Stevie, I was immediately knocked to the ground. My left leg burned and blood spread rapidly down my jeans. Glancing around without getting up, I spotted Stevie on the ground about ten yards in front of me. I couldn't tell if she was alive or dead, but she had obviously been shot. I lay as still as possible for what seemed like an eternity before the firing ceased and the afternoon was quiet again.

By the time I reached her body, Stevie was unconscious and her skin was white and cool from blood loss. As I said her name over and over, I saw that she had been hit at least three times. A military helicopter came into view and hovered near us as I tried to shield Stevie's body with mine. I barely remembered being evacuated to a hospital.

Two days later I was released from the hospital and preparing to return home. Stevie had been taken to Mexico City and then flown to Houston. The doctor wasn't sure whether she had survived or not, but even if she did, he was certain she would be paralyzed.

When I drove up to her cabin, I wasn't sure what to expect. Years had passed and I hadn't seen Stevie since her release from a Houston rehabilitation center. Her experience in Chiapas had changed her, and I had no idea what she was doing now or how she would greet me. As I looked around, everything seemed peaceful and very far removed from violence and the fast life.

The door to the cabin swung open and Stevie walked onto the porch. Now about forty, she still looked physically fit. She smiled when she saw me and stepped forward to hug me. As we embraced, I was glad to see that the doctors in Mexico had been wrong concerning her "certain" paralysis.

"It's good to see you again, Jo," she said.

"Been a while," I said.

"Well, come on in and take a load off," she said as she backed into her home.

The front hallway of her home was covered with pictures I knew she had taken on assignments. As we went down the hallway, I stopped and looked at a few of her pictures. She had a gift for capturing the emotion of the moment on people's faces.

"Remember this one?" she asked, pointing to a black and white.

I laughed when I saw it. "Was this in Chiapas?" I asked.

"Yeah, remarkably I got that camera back and this was on the last roll I shot. Cute, huh?"

There I was, frozen in time, aviator sunglasses pushed up on my head, smiling and holding an Indian child, both of us waving at the camera. It had been taken the morning of the military attack on the village, and I wondered what had happened to that child.

"I've looked better." I frowned.

"You were very cute," she said with a wink. "And happy."

"Long time ago."

I followed her into the living room and sat down on the couch.

"So what can I do for you, Jo?" Stevie asked as she sat in a recliner. "I know you don't make social visits."

"What are you up to these days, Stevie?"

"Not much. Teaching a few photography classes at the local community college. Pretty boring stuff. And you?"

"Retired."

"You? Never!" she exclaimed.

"Yep. Living back on my folks' ranch outside of Kerrville. For almost eighteen months now."

"I didn't think you'd ever leave the field."

"Well, sometimes Mother Nature takes care of that for us."

"I read that you were shot again at Kosovo." She frowned.

I smiled at her. "Yeah. After that I caught a break and did about three years of Stateside assignments. But then George W. decided to search for weapons of mass destruction. I was tapped to be embedded with a front-line unit in Iraq and decided that this old body couldn't handle much more lead, and it was time to do a walk-away. Besides, photojournalism is a young person's game."

"So what brings you to the boonies today then?"

"Do you remember me telling you about my son?"

"The one you adopted with your ex?"

"Yeah. He's gotten himself into a little trouble. He was working on a story and someone tried to kill him. I promised my ex that I would try to find out who might have been responsible. But the kid hates my guts because his mother and I separated, and I can't get close to him personally."

"And you need someone to get close and ask a few questions?"

"I'm not really sure what the story is. Seems like nothing, but there has to be something someone doesn't want found out. I need someone on the inside, Stevie."

"Is he a reporter?"

"In San Antonio." I nodded. "For the Light. Sammy Gomez is one of their photographers. I've talked him into taking a vacation for a couple of weeks."

"And you want me to poke around a little and see if anything turns up," Stevie said with a smile. "Why not? Getting a touch of cabin fever anyway."

Chapter
Nine

FOUR DAYS LATER, Stevie began working as a temporary employee of the San Antonio Light covering crime, which there would never be a shortage of. I booked adjoining rooms for us at the Marriott near the Riverwalk, figuring we might as well relax and enjoy ourselves as much as possible. There were plenty of good restaurants and bars along the Riverwalk, and even though Stevie was technically working, I hoped that getting out a little would help her reenter society. Every night she gave me a brief report on any information she thought might be useful. Admittedly, placing her at the Light was a long shot, but I was nearly at the end of my list of options without confronting Kyle directly. Stevie had been on the job nearly a week before Kyle returned to work.

"I can't believe I ever found this kind of work exciting," Stevie said after our waiter had taken our order for two thick steaks, medium rare. "I feel like a photographer for the coroner's office. I'm ready to see someone alive and kicking."

"Thinking of giving up photography?" I chuckled.

"Actually I've been thinking about moving over to outdoor photography. I've put out a few feelers to nature magazines," she said as she munched on a breadstick.

"Not very exciting, but there's money in it." I smiled. "Anything new today?"

"Kyle's back at work. I went on a gang shooting call with him this afternoon near the Old Market."

"How's he doing?" I asked as our waiter placed salads in front of us.

"Seems to be recovering pretty good," Stevie said,

stabbing at her lettuce. "From what I could tell he does a thorough interview."

"Did you mention his story?"

"Not in so many words." Stevie shook her head. "I told him I heard he had been shot covering a story, but he clammed up."

"Anyone else in the newsroom talk about it?"

"Just that he was shot. Apparently they have no idea what he was working on, and as far as I can tell, no one is associating his shooting with any story. They're all convinced it was a random incident."

"It could have been," I said. "I'm thinking this is all a waste of time."

"Well, I've got one more week to go. I'll do what I can, Jo."

"I know you will, Stevie."

"How is your ex anyway?"

The question surprised me and I shrugged. "Okay, I guess. I hadn't seen or talked to either of them for nearly fifteen years until Cate showed up on my doorstep a couple of weeks ago."

"You still carrying that torch?" She smiled.

"Well, she does look pretty damn good," I laughed. "Surprised the hell out of me that she contacted me."

"Thinking about rekindling your relationship?"

"No. No interest there anymore," I said even though I knew I was lying. "Besides, how do you know I don't already have someone at home?" I grinned.

"I know you, Jo."

"Yeah, well, I'm getting too old to be chasing after women."

"Bullshit!" Stevie exclaimed. "You're a damn fine-looking woman yourself, Jo. And remember, I've seen you in action."

BY WEDNESDAY OF Stevie's second week at the paper, we were no closer to Kyle's story than when we started. I had decided that if something didn't drop in our laps within the next day, we would pack it in. Late Wednesday afternoon, Stevie called and asked me to meet her at a bar named Jeri's, a few blocks from the newspaper.

Four or five Spanish tiled steps led down to the entrance

of Jeri's Bar and Grill. Refined wasn't the right word, but Jeri's wasn't what I had expected. Jim Beam tasted the same poured out of a brown paper bag or delivered in Waterford crystal. Jeri's seemed to pay quite a lot of attention to that intangible thing called ambiance. The minute I entered, I was met by an exquisite woman in her mid-forties — the kind anyone would like to see at the end of a rough day. She wore more makeup than I personally liked, but some things could be overlooked if other incentives were strong enough. I had always been attracted to taller than average women, and Jeri, who was barely half a head shorter than my own five-ten frame, certainly filled the bill.

"Hello," the woman said warmly in a husky voice. "I'm Jeri. Tell me what can I do for you today, sugar."

The greeting left itself open to a number of possible interpretations, and I wondered what Jeri's response would have been if she knew what was in my mind.

"I'm supposed to be meeting someone from the Light, darlin'," I finally said with a smile.

Jeri wrapped her arm around mine and led me away from the door. "You don't look like a reporter," she said, walking very closely next to me.

"Photographer." I smiled.

"Fascinating!" Jeri drawled. "Perhaps we can arrange for you to take a few pictures of me sometime. Privately, of course."

"I'm afraid I don't do portrait photography," I said.

"That's a pity. I'll bet you're really good at getting people to relax and act naturally for you," Jeri said, as she squeezed my arm.

Tiffany-style lamps were hung strategically around the room, casting a stained-glass glow onto the rich, wood-paneled walls. I noticed that there were a number of equally attractive women mingling with customers throughout the bar and was beginning to think a practical joke was being played on me when I saw Stevie at a candlelit table.

As I pulled out a chair and sat down, Jeri stood behind me. Placing her hands on my shoulders, she said, "What can I get you, sweet thing?"

"A beer. Imported if you have it."

Jeri massaged my shoulders as she asked Stevie whether she was ready for a refill.

Stevie leaned across the table after Jeri left. "Nice stuff, huh," she said.

I turned to watch Jeri walk away. "Not bad."

"They're all like her in here. Service with a smile."

"College students?" I asked.

"More like prostitutes," Stevie said over her glass. "But they can actually carry on an intelligent conversation about current events, and nothing ever goes on between the customers and the greeters."

"That's hard to believe. They're very attractive women," I observed.

"Therein lies the problem," Stevie grinned. "They're not women."

I had no idea what my expression must have looked like, but whatever it was seemed to make Stevie's day.

"No, shit," I said, looking around again.

Jeri returned with our drinks, and after setting them down, she rested a slender, well-manicured hand on my shoulder again. Whatever thoughts I might have been harboring about Jeri earlier were now completely flushed from my mind. That was what I got for lusting after another woman even if it was only in my mind. I had obviously been living alone too damn long and needed to take up dating again...soon.

After Jeri walked away, I said, "Hope that made your day, Stevie. That why you invited me to join you today?"

"It reminded me of that club we went to in Hamburg where all the women were transsexuals, but it's the first one I've seen around here," Stevie said.

"How'd you find this place?" I asked, still incredulous.

"The guys from the Light come here sometimes after work," she said. "In fact, they were here today. I thought you'd enjoy Jeri's and called you after they all left."

"Was Kyle here?"

"Yeah." Stevie chuckled. "Seems that once upon a time he almost had an intimate moment with one of the 'girls.'"

"Well, if they fooled a man, then I don't feel too bad about my reaction." I laughed as I took a drink.

"Your name came up," Stevie said.

"Oh, really."

"We were discussing overseas work, and when he found out I had been to Africa and Central America, he asked if I'd ever worked with you."

"And..." I prompted, leaning forward onto my elbows.

"And I told him you were a great journalist and the best lay I'd ever had." She shrugged.

"You what?" I choked out.

Throwing her head back, Stevie laughed. "Just kidding, Jo, except for the great journalist part." After a pause, she said, "Well, the other part is true, too, but I figured he probably didn't need to know that."

"Thank you," I said, relieved. "His opinion of me is bad enough without adding fuel to the fire."

"I'll tell you the truth, Jo," Stevie said, "I don't think I'm going to find out anything useful for you. It's like your son has lockjaw when it comes to talking about whatever he's working on. I've tried buddy-buddy and had him pretty much three sheets to the wind this afternoon and couldn't get jack out of him except about his girlfriend."

"Yeah." I sighed. "I think you're right. Maybe he's decided to dump the story."

"I know you'll disagree, but there isn't a story anywhere worth getting shot over."

"Neither of us used to think that way." I smiled.

"Well, maybe your son is smarter than we were."

Chapter
Ten

TWO LONG WEEKS had crawled by, and Stevie hadn't been able to find out anything about the story Kyle had been working on at the time he was shot, and I was becomimg convinced it was a dead end. Kyle and Sarita were going about their daily routines without even a hint of danger around them. I finally decided that it was time for Stevie to go back to her hideaway cabin when the photographer she was replacing came back from his vacation. I had gone through the pictures I had taken in Kyle's apartment a dozen times but still hadn't found anything useful or been able to decipher his shorthand. Pauli was at a dead end, too, and as far as I could tell there was nothing more to pursue. Kyle's shooting had to have been one of those random acts that were always in the news.

I was relieved to leave San Antonio and get back to my retirement. After all the assignments I had covered, all the dodged bullets, I couldn't remember doing anything more draining than the last three weeks in San Antonio. The only thing I wanted to do was return to the privacy of the ranch, but I felt obliged to tell Cate that I had come up with nothing.

I stepped off the elevator on the fifth floor of the Travis Professional Building in Austin at two-forty and walked toward a glass wall at the end of the hall. Bradley and Hammond was etched across the glass doors. Just inside was an oak-paneled reception area where a young woman was seated behind the desk. She was groomed for the secretarial fast track, and I was decidedly out of place in my jeans and denim work shirt. I left my sunglasses on as she turned toward me and smiled.

"Can I help you, ma'am?"

"Cathryn Hammond, please," I said as I glanced around the office. Cate must have decorated this part of the office herself, I thought. It was tastefully done and as understated as she was.

"Do you have an appointment?"

"Just tell her that Joanna Carlisle is here."

The woman picked up the phone and punched in a few numbers and waited. "Ms. Hammond? I'm sorry to disturb you. There's a lady here to see you. She doesn't have an appointment." She waited a moment and nodded as if the other party could see her. "She says her name is Joanna Carlisle." More nods and a glance at me. "Yes, ma'am. I'll tell her." She placed the receiver back in its cradle and smiled again. "Ms. Hammond asked that you wait a few minutes, Ms. Carlisle. She's just finishing up with another client."

I sat down on a couch at the opposite side of the reception room, rummaging through a few magazines on a glass coffee table. Fifteen minutes had passed when I heard Cate's voice. She accompanied her client into the reception area and stopped at the desk. She was wearing a fitted gray linen suit with a subtle white pinstriping. The collar of a white silk blouse was turned neatly over the collar of the suit jacket.

"Peggy, make an appointment for Mr. Douglas some time late next week." She turned to the client and placed a hand on his arm. Smiling, she said, "I don't think you have anything to worry about, Richard, but I'll know more after I've had a chance to check a few things."

"Thanks, Cate. This really takes a load off my mind."

They shook hands and good old Richard departed.

Cate turned toward me. "I'm sorry to keep you waiting, Jo. Please, come in." To Peggy, she said, "Hold my calls for about thirty minutes."

"You have another appointment in fifteen minutes, Ms. Hammond," the woman said, leafing through an appointment book.

"Just get them something to drink and apologize for me," Cate instructed. She moved down the hallway and stopped next to an open door. I entered the room, and she followed, closing the door behind her. "Coffee?" she asked as she walked to her desk.

"No, thanks," I answered. I sat down in a leather chair across from her and removed my sunglasses.

"Pauli and I have looked into every angle we could think of in San Antonio, but there just is no story there, Cate. Kyle might have been involved in something else, or the kid who shot him could have mistaken him for someone else."

"I see. Are you going to continue looking into it?"

"I'm on my way back to the ranch," I replied, shaking my head.

"He might still be in danger, Jo."

"He might or might not be." I shrugged. "But there isn't anything more I can do, Cate. I still don't know squat about what he's working on, and I can't spend forever tailing him, hoping to get a break."

"So you're just going to walk away?"

Now she was beginning to piss me off. None of this had been my idea to begin with, and her tone of voice made me feel like some kid who'd been called to the principal's office.

"Well, what would you like me to do?" I asked. "If you think this is so fucking easy then share some of your brilliant insights with me."

"You're the one who's supposed to have all the fabulous connections. Can't they do something?"

"They've already done everything they can. Look, I feel bad about leaving him to figure all this out by himself, okay, but that's what growing up is all about."

"Even if it gets him killed."

"Goddamn it, Cate. Do you want me to sleep in my car outside his apartment every night and guard him? He's a man. Let him be one, for Christ's sake."

She rose from her chair and glared at me. "I'm doing what any responsible parent should do when she finds out her child might be in danger. And you should, too, Joanna."

"In this case I think you're expecting too much."

"You're right, Jo. I used to expect you to be a parent and a partner, but you couldn't deal with that either."

Her words stung, and I felt blood rushing to my face as I stood to face her. "Don't throw that shit in my face! I can't change the past, okay."

"That still doesn't solve Kyle's problem."

"You asked me to help him, and I gave it my best shot. There's nothing to be found."

"Then maybe you should go back to the ranch and crawl into whatever hole you've dug for yourself. Forget you ever knew Kyle or me."

"I never knew him," I said through clenched teeth, "and I'm beginning to think I never knew you either."

Our discussion had degenerated into something much more personal. Years of built-up resentment and guilt had finally bubbled their way to the surface. We had had dozens of similar arguments during our years together, and our life had been either very good or very bad. Never anything in between. When we loved, we loved passionately. When we fought, we fought just as passionately.

"You weren't home long enough to know either one of us. Your idea of family responsibility was to leave for weeks or months at a time, come home and catch a fast night or two in bed, and then go back to whatever the hell you were doing without the slightest thought about whether we needed you or not."

"I don't remember having to work very hard to get you into bed, babe," I said with a sarcastic edge.

"I was your partner, Jo! I had to hope you remembered that between visits."

"Fuck you, Cate," I spat, pointing my finger at her. "You knew damn well what I did for a living when we met. I provided for you and Kyle every way I knew how."

"You gave us everything we wanted. Everything except yourself. I used to think you were consumed by your career, but now I know it was because you didn't give a damn about anyone except yourself. And fifteen years hasn't changed that."

During the course of our argument our voices had risen, apparently unnoticed by either of us. Cate had moved around her desk and was standing close enough that I had to restrain myself from smacking her just because it would have felt so damn good. She must have had the same idea because her hands were balled into fists. Whatever thoughts I was having were interrupted by a knock at the door. Before Cate could respond, the door opened partway, and a woman stuck her head into the room. She smiled at us uneasily.

"Do you need some assistance, Cate?" she asked with a quick look at me.

"No, Susan. Ms. Carlisle was just leaving."

Susan remained at the door and opened it further,

pulling wire-rim glasses from her face, and stared at me. I would have guessed that she was a few years younger than me, but the gray in her hair made it hard to tell.

I turned back to Cate and leaned closer to her. "Don't call me again."

Before she had a chance to respond, I turned and walked to the door. I stopped and glared at Susan until she moved away from the door. As I went down the hallway, I heard her ask, "Who the hell is that?"

"A dissatisfied former client." Cate's response was bitter.

Chapter
Eleven

I COULD'VE SLEPT in Wednesday morning, but I'd been restless since returning to the ranch. The sun was just beginning to break through the treeline in front of the house when I carried a cup of coffee out on to the front porch and settled into my father's favorite wooden rocker. Except for the chatter of a few birds and the repetitive squeaking of the rocker on the wooden porch, everything was peaceful.

The quiet of the morning was broken by the roaring sound of a car engine, and I squinted down the road leading to the house. A cloud of brown dust was billowing up from the unpaved road, and I knew Lena was on her way. I like being left alone but never got the hang of housekeeping. I hired Lena Rubio to come out once a week to dust, wash, and do other little household jobs. Wednesday was Lena's day in the country.

She was a no-nonsense woman of forty although she looked older. I hadn't asked many questions about her past and wasn't interested in credentials when I met her at a local bar. Best guess was that once upon a time she had been a real heartbreaker. Now she was usually a little overmade and hadn't missed many meals over the years. She always had an off-color joke to tell, smoked like a chimney, cussed like a sailor, and threw back drinks with the best of them. I'd met some rough-around-the-edges women in my life, and Lena ranked at least in my top ten most memorable women. But she had a heart of gold and was a sucker for anyone's sob story after a few beers.

Her old car slid to a stop near the porch, sending a cloud of dust toward me. I leaned against a porch post to wait as she hauled herself from the vehicle and had to smile when I saw her. Her black hair was piled haphazardly on top of her head with several strands falling down onto her face and neck. She reached into her car and pulled out a large fabric bag and slung it over her shoulder before slamming the car door shut.

"Rough night?" I asked as she trudged toward the front steps.

"Fuck you, Jo," she said as she continued up the steps and past me into the house.

From her response I knew immediately that she had overslept and hadn't had her coffee yet. I caught the front screen before it slammed shut and followed her into the kitchen. She threw her bag onto the kitchen table and grabbed a coffee cup from the cabinet next to the sink. When she turned around, I was already there with the pot of hot, black heart-starter. She shoved the cup toward me, and I poured. Carrying the cup to the table and sipping noisily as she sat, she stopped long enough to dig through the bag, finally fishing out a pack of generic cigarettes and a scratched-up Zippo lighter. She took a long drag on the cigarette as she snapped the lighter closed with a metallic click.

"God, I hate mornings," she said through exhaled smoke.

"Then come later. I don't give a shit when you get here," I said.

"Too damn hot later." She smiled at me, showing teeth that would have made an orthodontist drool. "Maybe I just move in here with you, sugar," she continued, squinting as smoke slowly rose over her face. "Then Lena won't have to worry about gettin' too hot...'cept maybe at night."

"Afraid I couldn't handle that one, Lena."

"You skinny women all alike." She laughed loudly. "Shit, I squash you like a bug in bed."

"But if you're any good, it'd be worth dying for, right?"

"Don't you worry youself 'bout that. Lena good enough. What you got today? Same as usual."

"Yeah, I haven't been back long enough to make much of a mess."

"It ain't like you use all the rooms or nothin'. Three, four at the most." She leaned toward me. "I tell you the truth, Jo. I a'most feel guilty 'bout takin' you money."

"I don't feel guilty about giving it to you, so what's the difference?"

"You know, some of the nosies in town are thinkin' you and me got somethin' goin' out here."

"Really?" I chuckled, remembering Cate's questions about Lena.

"You bet you ass. 'Fore long everbody gonna believe I'm Jo Carlisle's woman."

I had to laugh at the idea of the old-timers around Kerrville gossiping about me and Lena. Most of them hadn't seen me since I was eighteen and went off to college, although I liked to think I'd left one or two broken hearts behind when I left.

"No one believes that, Lena. You're too much woman for me," I said.

"You fuckin' right 'bout that."

She crammed the cigarette between her lips, picked up her coffee cup, and waddled into the laundry room behind the kitchen. As I left the kitchen, I could hear her singing to herself and water running into the washing machine. Lena was a good woman who had developed an unsavory reputation when she was younger and never bothered to set the record straight. She had never married and had no children. Most people regarded her as easy, and I had heard plenty of men bragging about being with her, but somehow I couldn't bring myself to believe everything I'd heard.

Half an hour later I was ready to go out the door. Lena was vacuuming the living room as I came down the stairs. She was wearing headphones and had a cheap cassette player clipped to the waistband of her polyester pants. In between pushes and pulls on the vacuum she undulated to whatever she was listening to. Watching her, I couldn't begin to imagine what kind of music could possibly inspire those particular movements. When I tapped her on the shoulder, she jumped nearly a foot, ripping the headphones off.

"You tryin' to give me a fuckin' heart attack, you stupid bitch! You shouldn't sneak up on a body like that."

"Didn't mean to scare you. I'm taking Jack out for a while. I'll be back in an hour or so."

"You think I give a damn where you go? Ain't like nobody ever calls or comes out here. You live like some kinda hermit anyway, like you 'fraid of folks. If you die, nobody know or care."

She pulled another cigarette out of her pocket. As I was

going out the door, I glanced back and saw she had resumed her dance with the vacuum cleaner.

When I moved back to the ranch, I sold off all the livestock except Jack. He still had some fight left in him but was reliable, and like me, getting too old to care about very much. We hadn't gotten off to a great start, and I doubted that a friendship would ever develop between us because we were both too accustomed to having our own way. But over the last year and a half, I came to admire his independent nature while he tolerated my stubbornness.

After lunch, I locked myself in the darkroom to develop some film I'd shot before I went to San Antonio on my Good Samaritan mission. I was in the middle of developing the first roll when Lena banged on the darkroom door.

"Jo! You got company!" she hollered through the door.

"Who the hell is it?" I yelled back.

"'Nother woman. You really be robbin' the cradle with this chica."

"I'll be out in a minute."

"Don't take all day. I ain't no hostess here."

Damn! The road to my house was turning into a tourist attraction. The advantage to living away from town was supposed to be that no one wanted to drive all that way just to visit.

No one was in the living room six or seven minutes later when I left the darkroom, and I thought maybe whoever it was had already left. As I entered the kitchen, Sarita Ramirez was sitting at the kitchen table with Lena, looking a little uncomfortable as she twisted a glass of tea in front of her. She stood up quickly when I came into the room.

"How are you, Miss Ramirez?" I said, going to the refrigerator and grabbing the pitcher of tea.

"Sarita, please. I'm sorry to intrude on you, Ms. Carlisle, but I really have to speak to you," she said.

"About what? Refill?" I asked, taking a glass from the cabinet next to the sink.

"No, thank you. I've spoken to Kyle's mother, and she told me she had asked you to help him. I wanted to tell you that I appreciated that. He's very stubborn, but he does need someone's help even if he doesn't want to admit it."

"I've done everything I can without knowing more about his story. I have to have a starting point."

"I can tell you what the story is. If you know that, will you help him?"

"Go ahead," I said as I poured tea into a glass and took a drink.

She glanced at Lena and then back at me.

"Would you prefer to go into my office?" I asked.

"It don't matter none, honey. She gonna tell me everthin' after you gone anyhow," Lena said with a chuckle.

Sarita blushed slightly and followed me to my office.

"Does Kyle know you're here?" I asked.

"No. I called in sick today after he left for work."

"If he finds out he might not be too happy that you came here."

"But he'd still be alive."

"You know that Kyle and I aren't on speaking terms, and I assume you know why," I said.

"Cate explained it to me, and I've seen pictures of the three of you together when he was a child."

"Have you ever asked him about them?"

"He doesn't discuss his past with me."

"All right," I said with a shrug, "tell me what you know."

"Before I moved to San Antonio and met Kyle, I taught school not far from here, in Mountain View, for a couple of years. It was a nice little town until ABP moved in."

"ABP?"

"American Beef and Pork. They bought the old meatpacking plant in Mountain View and expanded it. Almost as soon as they bought the plant, ABP started bringing in workers from someplace else and laying off the local workers who were in the union. The new workers are earning half what the union workers were."

I looked at her and shrugged again.

"Anyway," she continued, "the whole town changed almost overnight. Most of the workers hired by ABP were Hispanic and spoke virtually no English. In fact, the Hispanic population of Mountain View grew by nearly four hundred percent in the time I was there. Hispanic children flooded the schools, and the school district couldn't afford to fund a bigger bilingual program. They asked ABP for more tax money, but the company only made a one-time payment and refused to pay more."

"Is that why you left?"

"The workload became intolerable. I was the only Hispanic teacher in the school. Over time, in addition to my teaching duties, I was spending more and more time acting as a translator for administration as well as other teachers. It wasn't the money, and I don't mind hard work, but the town was becoming unsafe. There were a lot of assaults and burglaries. So eventually I decided to apply to one of the San Antonio school districts."

"Do you think these new employees are illegals?"

"They had to be, but most of the ones I spoke to about their children were eager to show me their papers. If they were fakes, there's no way I would have known."

"Did anyone report any of this to INS?"

"Of course, but when they finally came, they didn't find more than two or three illegals. Another teacher told me she had heard that most of the ABP employees didn't go to work that day. They may have been warned."

"Did the children stay in school all year?"

"No, there was a very large turnover of students."

"Do you know who does the hiring for ABP?"

"I think they use employment agencies. At least that's what I heard."

"I'd bet twenty bucks all the employment agencies are located in Eagle Pass or Del Rio with convenient branch offices in San Antonio." I smiled.

"I don't know anything about that."

"And this is what you told Kyle?"

"Yes."

"So where's the story? Just illegals is nothing, Sarita."

"They be buyin' them employees," Lena jumped in.

I hadn't noticed her standing at the door until she spoke.

"Eavesdropping again, Lena?" I asked with a smile.

"Some of my people worked for ABP two, three years ago. They the ones what got laid off to make room for them fuckin' illegals."

"If they've got papers, guess what, ladies, they're not illegals," I said.

"Shit, Jo, they ain't got no real papers. I can buy you papers today. How many you want?"

"And where would you get them?"

"San Antone. Cost you 'bout five hundred. There a woman who buys Social Security numbers from real people this side of the border. When you got that, you good to go."

"If these illegals are so damn poor, where are they going to get five hundred dollars?"

"Need eight to get to Mountain View. Costs another three for transportation. The company takes it outta their pay off the top."

"Hell, I can buy a bus ticket for eighty," I said.

"Not unless you got papers. Don't get no papers 'til San Antone."

"So I'm an illegal. I come across the border where I pay some coyote three hundred to drive me to San Antonio. Once I get there, I shell out another five for fake papers that get me on with no questions asked at ABP."

"You got the whole enchilada right there," Lena said with a smile.

"I wonder how many illegals make it to Mountain View through this pipeline," I said to myself.

"A bunch," Lena said. "Maybe fifty a month. Maybe more."

"They need that many workers?"

"The old plant only open five days a week with two shifts. ABP open six days a week, three shifts. Dangerous work so lots of 'em only last a coupla months. They ain't union, so the company lays 'em off at about six months anyway."

"Why?" Sarita asked.

"Saves a fortune on health benefits and pension plans," I said.

Lena smiled and nodded. "You got that right. My cousin who worked there pulled in fifteen or sixteen an hour. They bring in these illegals and pay them five max. A third the pay and no extras to worry 'bout."

"Jesus," I said as I grabbed a calculator from a desk drawer and punched in a few numbers. "If we figure that just one illegal making it to Mountain View earns around eight hundred a month, before taxes, the company is saving sixteen hundred on each non-union worker." Entering more numbers and watching the total grow, I exhaled a low whistle. "On fifty illegals, ABP could be saving eighty thousand per month for an annual savings of nearly a million dollars and that doesn't count what they save on benefits and pensions."

"It might be more than that," Sarita interjected. "I heard

Kyle say that the company was paying someone to find more employees."

"How much are they paying per employee?" I asked.

"I don't know," she answered.

Lena poked Sarita on the shoulder and smiled. "You need to work on that pillow talk, baby girl. Don't let no fool man fall asleep 'fore he tell you everthin' he know."

Sarita blushed again and looked back at me. "Do you think there's really a story here, Ms. Carlisle?"

"Maybe. I don't know much about this ABP. We used to sell our beef over at Mountain View, but that was when the old plant was open. I could look into a few things and see what turns up, Sarita. It could still be a zero story. But if I was raking in that kind of money, I might not want it getting out either."

Sarita picked up a piece of paper and took a pen from her purse. "This is my phone number at school," she said as she wrote. "I don't want Kyle to know I talked to you."

I took the paper from her and put it in my shirt pocket. "You be careful, too. If someone is watching him, they have to have seen you as well. Okay?"

She nodded and stood up. I walked around the desk and escorted her out of the house. As she drove away, I went back up the steps. Lena was leaning against the porch railing, smoking what was probably her fiftieth cigarette of the day.

"You gonna help you kid?" she asked.

"I said I'd look into it. Maybe I'll drive over to Mountain View tomorrow and poke around a little."

"Shit!" she exclaimed through a cloud of blue-gray smoke. "Ain't nobody there gonna talk to you. You the wrong cultural persuasion."

"Then I'll just have to find someone the right persuasion to help me out. I have a couple of friends in San Antonio who might do it."

"I do it. But it gonna cost you plenty extra." She smiled.

"You don't know anything about gathering evidence for an investigation, Lena."

"What the fuck you gotta know? How to ask some dumbass question? Shit, I got more questions than you got answers."

"Well, you're not going to do it. I won't allow it."

"What you mean you won't allow it? I do whatever I

damn please. Lena don't need no stinkin' permission from you."

"Then I won't pay you."

"I do it for nothin'. What you think 'bout that?"

"I wish you wouldn't, Lena," I said, changing tactics. "You could get hurt, and I sure as hell wouldn't want that on my conscience."

She slapped me on the back and laughed. "You like me, Jo. You ain't got no conscience. 'Sides, them fuckers put some a my people outta work. Make me real happy to bring 'em a little grief."

"Do you have a plan, or are you thinking about barging in with both arms swinging?"

"I figure I can get me a job where a buncha wetbacks might hang out. Give a man a few drinks and a nice smile, he tell you anythin'."

"If I go along with this, I want a report every day, and if I tell you to get out, you get your ass out, no questions asked. Deal?" I said, sticking out my hand.

She grabbed my hand so hard I thought she would break my fingers and pumped it up and down a couple of times before releasing it. "Deal. You know, that a real nice girl you kid got. He a dummy like you?"

"God, I hope not, Lena. I sure hope not," I answered as I flexed circulation back into my fingers.

Chapter
Twelve

I DIDN'T KNOW how she did it, but by the following weekend Lena Rubio was employed as a bar waitress and part-time cook at a Mountain View cantina six blocks from the ABP plant. You'd never be able to convince me that work was hard to find when a woman like Lena could just waltz into a place and get hired on the spot. Perhaps the cantina owner thought he could use her as a bouncer if he needed to. She was certainly large enough to take down most men I knew. She began a regular routine of going to work at the cantina in time for the lunch crowd and leaving around ten at night. The distance between Kerrville and Mountain View was about forty miles, and I provided Lena with gas money on a regular basis. She would drop by the ranch on her way to Mountain View and give me an amazingly detailed, if grammatically flawed, report of what she heard and saw each day, even arranging to take Wednesdays off from the cantina to clean my house.

Two weeks into her new job, Lena came by my house with her usual report. We shared a cup of coffee, and she somehow managed to chain smoke three or four cigarettes with it, looking preoccupied as she fidgeted around in her chair.

"Something wrong, Lena?" I asked.

"Naw. Think you can come to Mountain View t'night?"

"Sure. What time?"

"'Bout ten-thirty. Got somebody for you to talk to."

"You want to give me a little more to go on, or is it a national secret?"

"There this man I met. He says he knows plenty 'bout the ABP illegals."

"Do you trust him?"

"Hell, he so drunk most times, he might think ABP is how the fuckin' alphabet starts for all I know. You talk to him and see if he full of shit."

"Okay, I'll be there. Anything else on your mind? You seem a little jumpy."

"It's nothin'. Sometimes I get the feelin' somebody watchin' me, but ain't never nobody around."

"Maybe it's time for you to find another job and leave town."

"Ain't found nothin' yet. One more week. Gettin' tired of gettin' pawed by them stupid wetbacks anyhow."

She finished her coffee and lit another cigarette as she pushed herself up from the table. I followed her out of the house and watched her waddle toward her car.

"You be careful, Lena. Understand?"

"Yeah, yeah," she said with a dismissive wave of her hand.

All day I couldn't shake a nagging feeling that something was wrong. It wasn't like Lena to worry about anything. Maybe her feeling that someone was watching her was just the product of an overactive imagination. But then again, maybe it wasn't. I finally decided not to wait until ten-thirty to arrive in Mountain View. I needed to get the lay of the land anyway, and if experience served me right, most little Mexican cantinas usually had pretty good food as long as you didn't go in the back to personally inspect the kitchen. After checking my camera and loading it with high-speed ASA 800 film, I elected to forego the comfort of my Blazer in favor of my father's old ranch truck. No air conditioning or state-of-the-art stereo system, but it was old and faded enough that I hoped no one would be tempted to steal it. I hadn't driven it in a couple of months, but after a little coaxing, the engine finally turned over.

It had been years since I'd been to Mountain View, and I was surprised at the visible changes in the town. The city limits sign listed its population at 2,500, but even before I reached the downtown business district I knew they had undercounted. It was nearly six, and if what Lena had told me was true, one shift of workers would be leaving ABP in less than ten minutes. It didn't take a mental giant to find the meatpacking plant. All I had to do was follow my nose. There wasn't enough money in the world to entice me to inhale that odor day after day. As a teenager, I had helped my father take cattle to the Mountain View meatpacking plant, but the smell was stronger now than I remembered, probably due to the increased numbers of animals going through the plant.

As I drove around the perimeter of the plant, I saw that it had been enlarged considerably. Four large tractor-trailers were backed into a loading dock at the rear of the building, and as the pathetic bleating of animals going to slaughter penetrated the late afternoon air a shiver ran up my spine. Circling the block, I noticed a second loading dock with more trucks, many emblazoned with the names of large grocery chains on the side. One door in and one door out. Some of the workers had bragged to Lena about the volume of meat they were able to turn out on a single shift. Parking a block away from the main entrance to the plant, I waited for the shift to end. Nearly a hundred men and women were gathered outside the main gate waiting for the night shift to begin. Snapping a zoom lens onto my Minolta, I took a few quick shots of the workers. If the workers were illegals, they wouldn't be happy to know a stranger was taking their picture.

At precisely six, an armed guard opened the electric gate at the main entrance. A mass of men and woman began pouring out of the plant and headed eagerly for the gate, mingling briefly with the workers waiting to enter. From where I was sitting, it appeared that well over three-fourths of the workers were Hispanic and predominantly men. Their clothes looked filthy and were covered with reminders of their work. Groups of them passed by my car, carrying on animated conversations in Spanish. Once upon a time I had had a passable knowledge of street Spanish, but now I could only recall enough to catch an occasional phrase.

While I was struggling to pick up what I could, I noticed a white Lincoln Town Car, with the maximum window tinting allowed by law, pull up to the front gate. The vehicle nosed through a few workers and stopped, so the driver could speak to the guard before proceeding to a parking area near the front door of the building. A large, well-dressed man, who appeared to be Hispanic, got out of the car and looked around. He yelled something at some of the workers, and they moved a little more quickly into the plant. The man, still wearing sunglasses even though the sun had nearly dropped behind the building, proceeded into the building as I managed to take shots of his car. I would get Pauli to trace it through DMV for me later after I enlarged the license plate number.

Deciding to go to the cantina and play stupid white woman for a while, I started my truck and looked around to make sure there was no one coming before I pulled away from the curb, waiting as another tractor-trailer rumbled by. I hadn't seen it at first, but a metallic blue-gray Mercedes 380 SL was following the truck. Shit, I thought. If I had hit that sucker, my insurance premiums would have doubled overnight. The Mercedes stopped briefly at the plant gate, and the guard waved it through. As I watched, it pulled in next to the Lincoln. Refocusing my camera, I snapped off a couple of shots of the Mercedes. The driver of the Lincoln came out of the plant entrance and walked to the driver's side of the Mercedes, leaning down and speaking to whoever was driving. Finally, the car door opened, and the second driver got out, but my view was blocked by the Hispanic man as they walked back into the plant.

After waiting for a second tractor-trailer to pass, I made a quick U-turn and drove toward Rafael's Cantina. The cantina was a stand-alone building squeezed in between two larger buildings, and all three looked run down. No pride of ownership here. Fiesta lights hung under a faded striped awning, which was held up by dented aluminum poles. I had no trouble finding a parking space near the cantina and guessed that most of the workers who frequented the businesses along the street couldn't afford vehicles. In fact, the only things on wheels that I had seen worth owning were the two that had pulled into the ABP parking lot. Throwing my jacket over my camera case, I looked around inside the truck to make sure there wasn't anything in sight that might entice someone to break in.

As I got out, a small group of four or five men walked past my truck, speaking in subdued voices and glancing at me out of the corners of their eyes. Illegals almost never looked directly at you, thinking perhaps that someone could tell they were illegal by simply looking into their eyes. Two of the men turned into the cantina while the others kept walking.

Rafael's Cantina was pretty much what I had expected. I'd been in a hundred places like it before, and whether they

called it Rafael's Cantina, Omar's Casbah, or Hans'
Biergarten, they were basically all the same—poorly lit,
smoky places where men and whores hung out trying to get
a cheap drink, or a cheap trick, or both. Although there were
bare light bulbs scattered around the room, they couldn't
have been more than twenty or thirty watts each.
Approximately twenty men were gathered around the bar
working on brown and green bottles of beer. A hand-lettered
sign over the bar advertised the finest Old Mexico had to
offer in the way of beer and announced a special on tequila.
I was adjusting to the dim lighting and looking for a place to
sit when I heard a familiar voice.

"Lookin' for a seat, sugar?" Lena said.

I nodded, and Lena lumbered off, motioning for me to
follow her. I was amazed at the ease with which she
negotiated her way around the cramped tables and loose
hands. She stopped on the far side of the room next to a
vacant booth and waited for me to reach her. I slid into the
booth and waited for a menu.

"What can I getcha?" she asked without producing a
menu.

"What do you recommend?" I asked with a smile.

"I don't recommend nothin' in this dump, 'cept maybe
the beer, and it's only lukewarm."

"Got any enchiladas?"

"Yeah, but Rafael did the cookin' today."

"Then bring me that and a Corona Light with a twist of
lime."

"What you doin' here so early?" she asked in a low
voice as she wrote down my order.

"Didn't have anything else to do so I thought I'd check
out the town while it was still light."

"How you figurin' to kill four hours? Ain't like we got
no floor show or nothin'."

"I'll just observe and see what turns up."

"Only thing likely to turn up in here is more
cockroaches."

She left with my order and returned with the beer a few
minutes later. She had been right about its being lukewarm,
but it was wet.

"You stick out over here like a sore thumb. You so
white, you practically glowin' in the dark."

"I'll try to sit farther back in the shadows." I chuckled

Before we could say any more she was off again. I watched her work the room, laughing and talking to some of the other customers who seemed to honestly enjoy her company. A couple of them had already reached their quota of beer and made clumsy grabs at her ass, which she managed to deflect with a laugh. When she reached the bar, she handed an order sheet to a dark, unsmiling Hispanic man. He looked middle-aged, but most of his face was obscured by shaggy black hair and a mustache that needed trimming. It drooped down the sides of his mouth, giving him a perpetual frown. He handed her a tray full of beer and food, which she dropped off at various tables before setting a large plate of steaming enchiladas down in front of me.

"You wanna 'nother Corona?" she asked.

"Yeah, why not."

"Don't burn your tongue," Lena said as she turned to walk away. Stopping, she looked at me over her shoulder. "You find anythin' crunchy in them enchiladas, just keep chewin' and wash it down quick. Otherwise it might crawl back up."

Although there had been a smile on her face when she said it, I was tempted to examine the enchiladas more closely before taking a bite.

By ten-thirty, my truck was the only vehicle parked along the street. I had been killing time outside for nearly forty-five minutes when I saw Lena leave the cantina, accompanied by an older Hispanic man who waited for her before walking up the street toward where I was parked. I got out and leaned against the hood, waiting for Lena to make whatever introduction needed to be made. The man looked like he was about my age, mid-fifties, and he never stopped looking around. He hesitated as they got closer to me, and Lena reached out and grabbed his shirt to move him forward.

"This is Juan," she said as she thrust him toward me. His eyes were cast to the ground, and I knew he was an illegal.

"Juan Doe, I suppose," I said with a smile, but the remark sailed over both their heads.

Juan glanced up at me cautiously without speaking.

Nudging him, Lena ordered, "Tell her what you tol' me. She don't give a shit if you an illegal."

"I worked at ABP," he said with a fairly heavy accent.

"You don't work there now?" I asked.

He shook his head. "They laid me off when I got hurt."

"How did you get hurt?"

He pulled a hand out of his jeans pocket and held it up in the light for me to see. The ends of four of the fingers on his left hand were missing, and there was a red, swollen scar across the palm of his hand. From the looks of it, I estimated that the damage had probably happened a month or so before. As soon as I had seen his hand, he plunged it back into his pocket.

"How did it happen?"

"Saw. The chain it move too fast."

"They hang the meat from a movin' chain. Then increase the speed of the chain to increase production," Lena said matter-of-factly.

"I'm sorry about your hand, Juan. Can you tell me how you got your job at ABP?"

He nodded and looked around again. "I come across border with other men from my village. A man, he take us to San Antonio where we get papers saying we can work here. Then he bring us here."

"How much did you have to pay?"

"Eight, nine hundred American dollars. Now I got nothin'. No money, no job."

"Do you know the names of the people you paid the money to?"

He shook his head. "Only the man who speaks for ABP."

I looked at him and waited.

"Tell her the name," Lena ordered.

"Felix Camarena. He hire workers for ABP."

"Did you meet him in Mexico?"

"San Antonio. He bring papers to us and give money to the coyote for us."

"He paid the coyote after you paid the coyote?"

"Si...yes."

"You've mentioned this Camarena guy a few times in your notes," I said to Lena. "Did you get his name from other workers besides Juan here?"

"They all know Camarena. He don't work at ABP. They hire him to bring illegals in," she answered.

"They hired him to bring workers in," I corrected. "There's still no proof the company knows they're illegal."

"Then them people runnin' ABP are stupid. You think there just be workers layin' around dyin' to work in that stinky place?"

"Maybe they think they're illegals, but don't want to ask too many questions about where Camarena finds them."

Lena poked Juan again and said, "Tell her 'bout your brother."

"He work for ABP, too."

"Will he talk to me?"

"He in 'Braska."

"Nebraska?"

"Yes. Big plant there. Bigger than this. Many men from my village go there."

"And they all came through San Antonio and Camarena?"

"Yes."

While I was pondering what Juan had just told me, a car moved up the street toward us causing Juan to jump back into the shadow of the closest building and press himself against the wall as if hoping to blend in with the aging bricks. I glanced around and saw the white Town Car I had seen earlier at the ABP plant. As it passed, it appeared to slow down momentarily before speeding up again and moving down the street away from us. When my attention returned to Juan, he was still in the shadows.

"I go now. Can't stay here," he said.

"What's wrong with you?" Lena asked him.

"Camarena," he said, looking in the direction of the Town Car. Before I could ask another question, he slipped around the corner of the building and disappeared into the darkness.

I had gotten the message and looked at Lena. "Looks like this was your last day slinging beer and enchiladas around the old cantina. Get in your car and I'll follow you. I hope Rafael isn't expecting two weeks' notice."

Chapter
Thirteen

I SPENT THE following two days in San Antonio digging into the background of ABP. They were one of the Big Three meatpackers in the United States and ran their business in a way that would have made Upton Sinclair proud. They had large meatpacking plants in five Midwestern states. In every case, they bought out local meatpackers and expanded the plants, produced around the clock, and eliminated union packers, giving me a new appreciation for the meat at my local grocery store.

ABP and the other big meatpackers were bringing in eighty billion a year in meat sales and had recently diversified into prepackaged meats and the overseas markets. Asian markets, in particular, were ripe for American beef, and ABP had been one of the first to tap into that potentially huge market. Elementary math got me into bigger numbers than I knew existed. ABP, and probably the other big packers, were shelling out a small fortune for workers. Someone was getting that money plus what the workers themselves paid to enter the country illegally. Millions were exchanging hands in order for the companies to make billions. I could see why someone had wanted to stop Kyle, or anyone else, from digging into the story, and I felt the familiar thrill of investigating a story returning.

I made copies of information I found on microfilm, mostly old newspaper articles about the ABP buyout in Mountain View. Other than a couple of stories about how the community had benefited from having a large company in their midst, the company had managed to keep a relatively low profile.

I was packing my bag Friday morning, preparing to

return to the ranch, when I decided to call Sarita.

"Ventana Middle School," a woman answered in a bored voice.

"Yes, ma'am. I'd like to leave a message for Ms. Ramirez."

"Which one?"

"Sarita Ramirez."

"She's in class now, but I can put a message in her box."

"Tell her that Joanna Carlisle called. If she wants to talk to me, I'll be at the Holiday Inn near Santa Rosa Medical Center until just after lunch. Room four sixteen."

"I'll give her the message," the woman barely got out before disconnecting me.

I had absolutely no idea whether Sarita would call me back or not but figured I should let her know that I hadn't ignored her request. I finished packing what few clothes I had with me and lay back on the bed to look over the material I had found. Less than half an hour later, the phone next to the bed rang.

"Hello," I said.

"Ms. Carlisle? This is Sarita. I just got your message."

"I wanted to let you know I was in town. I've been doing some background research, and I'm leaving for the ranch this afternoon."

"Can we meet before you leave?"

"Uh, sure. When do you get off work?"

"I don't want to delay your trip home. I'm off for lunch right now and have a conference period after that, about an hour and a half."

"Well, if you give me directions to your school, I'll stop and pick up something for lunch and meet you there."

Ventana Middle School was close to the apartment building where she and Kyle lived, so I wasn't totally lost and arrived within half an hour. Following her directions, I entered the school through a side door on the east side of the building and saw Sarita standing in the doorway of a classroom waiting for me. She closed the door behind her as I set the bag of food on a worktable near the rear of the room and pulled out a couple of wrapped burgers. She brought an extra chair to the table and patted me on the shoulder as she sat down.

"It's good to see you again, Ms. Carlisle. I wasn't sure if my visit had been successful or not."

"It probably wouldn't have been if it weren't for my housekeeper."

"Ms. Rubio?"

"Yeah, she twisted the knife in my back until I agreed to at least do some background work."

"She seems to be a very interesting lady."

"That's a diplomatic description," I said as I took a bite.

Sarita laughed lightly. "I just mean that she seems like the kind of woman who would be willing to do anything for a friend."

"She helped me get enough information to know Kyle's got a potentially huge story. For his safety, as well as yours, he might need some help, Sarita." I reached into my pocket and pulled out a slip of paper. "These are the names of a couple of people who know how to get things done and aren't interested in taking any credit for the story. Whoever's behind this scheme isn't going to let one reporter get in their way, but if three or four have to be eliminated they might decide it isn't worth the risk and back off."

"What did you find out?"

"Enough to know there's a lot of money involved. People have been killed for a lot less."

"I wish he would let you help him."

"The chances of that are slim and none, Sarita."

"You know, Ms. Carlisle, Kyle is like you in many ways. Smart, but very stubborn."

"Well, right now he better be working on plain old scared. Whoever is involved won't let one reporter ruin a good thing. If he gets in their way, they'll kill him."

By late afternoon, I was on the road back toward Kerrville. Sarita had been right about Kyle and me. We were both stubborn, with a nearly self-destructive need to work things out alone. I had spent the last fifteen years going it alone, and only recently realized it hadn't been a particularly happy journey, even if I had been satisfied with the work. Or at least I thought I had been. It was hard not to think about what my life would have been like if I had been less...less what? I could spend the rest of my life wondering about that and never arrive at an answer. Too bad you can't see what's on the road ahead, so you'd know when to pull over for a U-turn and when to accelerate toward it.

The distance between San Antonio and Kerrville wasn't far enough for much self-psychoanalysis, thank God. I was too tired to think about what might have been or should have been and didn't want anything except a long, hot shower before falling into my own bed.

Only the final remnants of sunlight remained on the horizon by the time I turned into the drive leading to my house. Low mesquite blocked my view until the second curve on the gravel and dirt road. As the number of trees decreased, I caught sight of my house for the first time and saw that there was a light on inside. It was Friday and no one should have been there. Instinctively, I took my foot off the accelerator and let the car continue rolling forward, but there was enough gravel on the road to make it nearly impossible to approach the house without being heard. Rounding the last curve and breaking into the open clearing that became the front yard, I saw Lena's car parked in front of the house. I looked around the remainder of the property and wished the sun would hang in the sky a few moments longer. I didn't see any other vehicles anywhere and thought maybe Lena had something important to tell me and decided to wait around until I got home. Shrugging off my unease as paranoia, I got out of the car and grabbed my bag from the backseat. If Lena was waiting for me, I could expect a tongue-lashing for keeping her waiting so long.

From the foot of the porch steps I could see that the front door was ajar. The light I had seen wasn't coming from the front room but appeared to be from the window in my office. I took the steps two at a time and pushed the door farther open, looking into the darkened living room. Even in the growing darkness, I knew someone had been there and possibly still was. I was afraid to call out Lena's name and wished I had a weapon. Setting my bag down inside the front door, I caught the screen to keep it from slamming shut. Every piece of furniture had been thrown around the living room. Broken pieces of glass from the end table reading lamps crunched under my feet. Otherwise, the silence was overwhelming.

"Lena?"

There was no answer, and I went to the kitchen doorway and glanced in. Dishes and pots were strewn on the floor. Several beer bottles were sitting on the kitchen table and appeared to be the only unbroken items in the room. Anger, mixed with fear, was beginning to work its way into my mind, but by then I was convinced that whoever had been in the house was no longer there, or I would have already been attacked.

Raising my voice a notch, I called out again, "Lena!"

Subconsciously, I knew the rest of the house had also been trashed, but where the hell was Lena? The only light came from the partially opened door of my office, and I crossed the living room toward it. Standing to one side of the door, I took a deep breath and pushed the door open with one hand and scanned the office from one side to the other before entering. If possible, the office was in worse shape than the living room and kitchen. Other than the mess, there was nothing else in the room.

As quickly as I could, I searched the rest of the rooms. There was still no sign of Lena, and I began to hope that she hadn't been able to start her old car and had gotten a ride home from a friend. Going back into the living room, I switched on the overhead light and looked for the phone. My hand was shaking from an adrenaline overdose caused by a combination of fear and anger as I dialed.

"Sheriff's department," a man's voice answered.

"This is Joanna Carlisle, out on Route Fifty-four. My house has been broken into."

"Do you know how long ago, ma'am?"

"No. I've been out of town for a few days and just got back. But my housekeeper's car is here."

"Can your housekeeper identify the intruder?"

"I haven't spoken to her yet. She might not have been here. Look, just send a car out here."

"Someone should be there in ten or fifteen minutes."

I hung up and wondered if they had left any beer in the refrigerator. Flipping on the kitchen light, I went toward the refrigerator, but before I could open it, my hand froze on the handle. Lena's fabric bag was lying on the floor not far from the kitchen table. She was still here someplace, but I had already looked everywhere in the house.

Going onto the porch, I went down the steps toward her car. The doors were locked, but when I looked through the side windows, I didn't see anyone inside. I stood for a few minutes with my hands on my hips and looked around. Finally, taking a high-beam light from the rear storage area of the Blazer I walked around the outside of the house, shining the flashlight into the trees and bushes that enclosed the yard. By the time I returned to the front of the house, I wondered whether whoever had been here had taken Lena with them.

Sitting down on the porch steps to wait for the sheriff's deputies to arrive, I leaned back and looked up. There wasn't a cloud in the sky, and stars were beginning to appear, as the sky grew darker. When I was a kid, I had loved to lie in the grass and look straight up at the stars. After a few minutes it had seemed that I was floating in them, giving me a touch of vertigo, but at the same time, a detachment from reality and the magical feeling of floating among the stars. The thought brought a smile to my face, and I lowered my eyes back to Earth and scanned the front yard. From the corner of my eye the barn and corral loomed in the darkness. My stomach tightened into a knot, and faster than I thought I could, I sprinted toward the barn. The door leading to the stall area was open, and I flipped on the flashlight as I approached the door. It was quiet, but it shouldn't have been. Jack would have heard me coming, but there was no greeting from him. Standing in the doorway, I shined the beam down the passageway in front of the stalls. Halfway down the walkway, my worst fear was confirmed.

Lena's body was strapped to an open stall gate; her arms spread crucifixion style, and her feet tied to the bottom rail of the gate. The ropes that held her sagging weight had burned and cut the skin on her upper arms and her head dangled under a disheveled mass of black hair.

"Lena!"

She didn't answer me as I lifted her head. I had to close my eyes to avoid looking at her. I grabbed a pair of tin snips to cut the rope around her feet. Then, trying to hold her body upright against mine, I began cutting the ropes holding her arms. When I finally managed to cut through the last rope, the dead weight of her body nearly caused me to drop her. She was a big woman, over two hundred pounds, but now that weight had been increased as it became inert. As gently as I could, I laid her down and pushed her hair out of her face. Blood had run from her mouth and nose and was partially dried, and the rest of her face swollen into a grotesque shape. I tried to feel for a pulse but couldn't find one.

"Lena!"

In desperation, I ripped her shirt open and pressed my ear tightly against her chest. It might have been my imagination, but I thought I felt a heartbeat. I picked up the flashlight and looked around until I found a rag. I went quickly to the water hose and wet the rag to clean her face. As I rushed back to Lena's side, the light in my hand flashed momentarily into Jack's stall, and I stopped. A huge lifeless mass lie on the floor. I saw that his throat had been slashed, and his once beautiful body had already begun to bloat. No matter how much I wanted to help him, I knew there wasn't anything I could do, and I returned to Lena's side.

Wiping blood from her face as gently as I could, I spoke to her in whispers. An eternity later she produced a low moan, and I continued talking to her, hoping she could hear me. In the midst of my talking, I heard a car in my drive and looked up in time to see a sheriff's unit coming to a stop in front of the house, red and blue lights flashing.

Waving the flashlight toward them, I yelled, "Down here! Call an ambulance!"

An instant later the unit was driving over the grass toward the barn. I was glad not to be alone and helpless anymore. As I watched the car come toward us, a hand grabbed my shirt and nearly gave me a heart attack. It was Lena's hand, as strong and powerful as ever, pulling me toward her until her mouth nearly touched my ear.

"Who did this Lena?" I asked.

"Four spics," she managed through swollen lips.

Pulling my head up, I looked at her and wiped her forehead.

"Did you know them?"

She shook her head slightly, and something that might have been a smile crossed her swollen mouth. "This gonna cost you plenty extra," she rasped.

Chapter
Fourteen

LENA DIED IN the ambulance, clinging to my hand, and it took me hours to get away from the sheriff's deputies. The assholes said it was probably someone hopped up on drugs and looking for money. Drugged-out psychos, my ass. I knew why Lena had been killed even though I didn't have a shred of evidence to prove it. I felt responsible for her death. I should have known what could happen. Someone was going to pay for what they had done, and I didn't care if I had to kill the s.o.b. myself.

By the time a sheriff's car took me back to the ranch, I couldn't stand the thought of being there. The inside of the house was a disaster, and the sheriff's investigators would only make it worse. I couldn't shake visions of the struggle that must have taken place there from my mind. Although I had taken hundreds of pictures dealing with death and dying, violent death had never struck so close to me before. This time I wouldn't be able to turn and walk away as I always had. For now I needed to forget what I had seen that night and had to get the hell away from there. Knowing I wouldn't be able to get Lena's face out of my mind without help, I pulled into an all-night convenience store on the edge of town.

How I got there without killing myself or getting pulled over I don't know, but a little after two in the morning I lurched to a stop in front of Cate's house in Austin. It was dark and for a while I sat in my car, finishing the last of the twelve-pack I bought in Kerrville. Too much beer too fast on an empty stomach had given me a thundering headache, but even that was better than thinking about Lena's face and imagining the pain she had endured because of me.

I pushed the car door open and the rush of cool fresh air, combined with suddenly standing up, caused me to stumble. As I rested against the hood of the Blazer to regain my balance, I looked toward Cate's house. It wasn't what I had expected. Thought she'd have a real mansion, but it was an average-looking split-level ranch-style. A guard light over the garage lit up the front of the house; and it was a damn good thing or I'd never have made it to the front door. I pushed the doorbell and kept pushing it until an inside light came on. The front door cracked open, and I felt proud of myself for waking Cate up from a peaceful sleep. Why should she be enjoying herself on a night like this? I sure as hell wasn't.

"Jo? What the hell are you doing here?"

"We have to talk."

"You're drunk." She frowned. "Come back if you sober up."

"No! Now!" I shouted. "Open the fuckin' door!"

"Will you shut up before the neighbors call the police?"

"Let 'em! You know I don't give a shit about the police!"

The front door closed, and I banged on it with my fist.

"Open this door, goddamn it!"

The door finally opened, and I pushed against it before she could change her mind. I pushed harder than I needed to, and the door flew open, sending me sprawling onto the entryway floor. She moved my legs out of the way and closed the door. Leaving me there, she went down a hallway into another room. I can't be certain how long I lay there before she returned, and I felt her hand on my arm.

"Get up, Joanna."

"I can't."

"If you don't get up, I'll let you lie there the rest of the night."

I rolled over and tried to look at her but couldn't get my eyes to focus properly. I sat up slowly and tried to take a deep breath. More air didn't help, and I knew my body was swaying.

"The fuckin' floor is moving," I said.

"How much have you had to drink?"

"Obviously not enough. I'm still conscious," I answered.

She took my arm, and eventually I was able to stand.

With a little help from the walls and various pieces of
furniture, I made my way into the living room. Cate took my
arm again, attempting to lead me to the couch, but I jerked
away from her.

"Just leave me the fuck alone," I said, holding my arms
up. "This is all your fault anyway. You just couldn't leave
me the fuck alone."

"Jo..." she began.

"Lena's fuckin' dead!" I said, pointing at her. "And it's
your fault."

"What?"

"Listen, damn it. Lena's been murdered. If you'd stayed
out of my life, she'd be alive right now," I accused. "But no,
you just had to butt into Kyle's business, and she paid the
price! I'm alive, you're alive, Kyle's alive. But she's lying on
a slab in the fuckin' morgue. Didn't even make it to the
fuckin' hospital. Shit!"

"I'm sorry, Jo. Sit down."

I fell onto the couch and didn't hear her leave the room.
When she returned, she tapped my arm and handed me a
cup of coffee.

"I don't want that."

"Maybe not, but you need it."

"What is it? Some of that fancy French vanilla hazelnut
shit." As I took the cup, she kept her hands close to it in case
I couldn't keep a grip on it.

"Do you know what happened?"

"She was trying to help. Someone found out. They killed
her. End of Lena. End of story."

"Did she tell you who did it, Jo?"

"Don't you think that if I knew that, I'd have killed the
son of a bitch already?" I was angry, frustrated at being
interrogated. My eyes burned as I tried to ward off tears.

"Who was she trying to help?"

"Kyle."

"How..."

"The woman didn't even know him and ended up
giving her life for his stupid fuckin' story. Shit!" I mumbled,
fighting the tears that were forming in my eyes. "She did it
to help me."

Cate sat down on the couch next to me and put her hand
on my shoulder. "I'm so sorry, Jo."

"What the hell are you sorry about? You didn't know

her. She was a nobody. A nothing."

"She must have been a good woman for you to have cared about her."

I set the coffee cup carefully on a table and rubbed my face with both hands. I could feel her hand on my shoulder.

"Don't touch me. I don't want you to touch me. Lena's dead because of you," I said, even though I knew it wasn't true.

"Why don't you lie down and sleep it off," she said as she let her hand slide from my shoulder.

"I don't want to sleep. I don't want to dream about any of this. It's a fuckin' nightmare."

She stood up and I leaned back on the couch with my eyes closed.

"I wish things had been different. I wish I could have been a different person. Then maybe none of this would have happened," I said.

"I don't think you could have changed, Jo," she said quietly. "You wouldn't have been you anymore."

"Remember how we used to be?" I asked, half to myself. "I couldn't look at you without wanting you. I'd never met a woman as beautiful as you," I mumbled as I lay down slowly. I felt myself drifting toward sleep and was trying to fight it with the sound of my own voice even though it was beginning to trail off.

"Don't talk. Try to rest," she whispered.

I grabbed her arm and tried unsuccessfully to blink clear vision back into my eyes to look at her. "God, Cate, I loved you so much. I wish...you knew."

As my eyelids lost their battle with fatigue, I barely heard her say, "I knew, Jo, but it wasn't enough."

She brushed my hair back with her fingers, and the feel of her hand on my hair made me feel safe and comfortable for the first time I could remember in fifteen years.

WHEN MY EYES opened again, I tried to adjust them to the darkness, not sure where I was. My head pounded when I tried to sit up, and my tongue had Velcroed itself to the roof of my mouth. There was an afghan draped across me, and it almost won the battle as I tried to throw it off. My eyes strained in the dark to find my shoes. I didn't remember removing them, but then I didn't remember much

about the previous evening after finding Lena. The only
sound I could hear was a clock ticking somewhere. From the
sound of it, it must have been a very large clock, or I had
consumed more alcohol than I thought I had. I felt the
pockets of my jeans and found my car keys. When I reached
the Blazer and turned on the ignition, the clock on the dash
told me it was a little before six. The sun would be up before
I got back to the ranch.

As the Blazer came around the final curve leading to my
house, I saw two sheriff's vehicles parked on the lawn. A
tow truck was backed up to Lena's car, and a middle-aged
man in overalls was hoisting the rear end of the car in the
air. I had no idea where they would take it or who would
come forward to claim it, and I wished I had asked Lena
more questions about her family. As I approached the house,
a deputy I didn't recognize came onto the porch. Yellow
police tape superficially blocked the entrance to the living
room, and the deputy held the tape up as I ducked under it.

"Are you all right, Ms. Carlisle?" he asked.

"Yeah, great," I lied as I walked into the house.

If anything it looked worse than I remembered. The
cushions on the couch and chairs had been slashed, and
other furniture was overturned. It was hard to tell what had
been damaged by the search of the house, and how much
had resulted from the struggle that must have occurred.
Lena was a strong woman, and I knew she hadn't gone down
without a helluva fight. The investigators hadn't helped
either, spreading black fingerprint powder everywhere. I
wandered into the kitchen and was glad to see that the
coffee maker had escaped intact. I leaned against the counter
and waited as coffee filled the pot. A few cups later, the
deputy came into the kitchen.

"We're about finished here, Ms. Carlisle."

"Fine," I said without enthusiasm.

"Are you planning to stay out here?"

"No place else to go. When can I clean up this mess?"

"Well, I think we've done all we can in the house. Just
don't do anything in the barn until we can finish gathering
up whatever there is to find there."

"Guess I won't have any reason to be in the barn now,"
I said, remembering the sight of Jack's body lying in his
stall.

"It looks like whoever did this was looking for

something. If they didn't find it, they might come back," he warned.

"They didn't find anything. There wasn't anything here to find."

"Do you have a weapon, ma'am?"

"Yeah, and I know how to use it."

"You might want to stay someplace else, at least for tonight."

"Thanks, but I'll be fine."

"We'll have a unit swing by here after dark, just in case."

"Appreciate it."

Ten minutes later everyone was gone, and I was alone with a monumental mess. I had left the house and everything in it basically the same as my parents had always had it. The only changes I had made since making it my home was converting a downstairs guestroom into a darkroom and redoing the office to make it more suitable for my needs. It was almost as if I had been trying to hang on to their memories by not changing too much. Now some bastard had felt the need to destroy those memories along with the furniture.

It was after two in the afternoon before I stopped picking things up. The furniture was still a mess, but at least it was all upright again, and most of the fingerprint powder was cleaned up. Whoever had torn things up had missed the hidden storage area in the office floor where I kept a rifle and shotgun. Checking to make sure they were loaded, I leaned them against a wall where they could be reached quickly if I needed them. I was preparing to tackle my office when I heard the sound of a car. Grabbing the rifle, I went to the front door and looked down the road until a car I recognized came into sight. I pushed the screen door open and stepped onto the porch, leaning my rifle against the front doorjamb.

Cate got out of her car and saw me standing on the porch. As I watched her walk toward me, I couldn't help but notice that she hadn't gain an ounce since the day I first met her.

"What are you doing here?" I asked as she came up the steps toward me.

"I thought you could use some help. Were you expecting someone else?" she asked, glancing at the rifle.

"Whoever was here could come back for another look. They were probably looking for me instead of Lena anyway."

I picked up my rifle and opened the screen door for her. She stopped just inside and shook her head.

"Pretty messy," I said.

"Where are you working right now?"

"I thought I'd see what I can do in the office. It's pretty much trashed."

I felt her hand on my arm. "Are you going to be all right?"

"I'll adjust. I always have."

We went into the office, and I began picking up papers from the floor. Cate left the room and returned with a bucket of water and sponges. We worked without talking for nearly an hour.

Finally I said, "Let's take a break."

She dried her hands on her jeans, and I went into the kitchen and poured coffee for us. We carried our cups onto the front porch to take in some fresh air and clear the disaster inside from our minds.

"Do you want to talk about it, Jo?" she asked.

"No," I answered without looking at her.

"You can't keep your feelings bottled up inside. Sooner or later they're going to come out."

"You know, Cate, I don't recall seeing a psychology degree hanging in your office when I was there."

"I don't understand why you won't let anyone get close enough to help you."

Shifting my eyes toward her, I said, "Because when you let someone get too close you eventually wind up hurting her or getting hurt yourself."

"You want a refill?" she asked as she got up.

"Why not," I said, draining my cup before handing it to her.

While she was gone, I got up and stretched. I heard the sound of gravel being crushed under car tires again and quickly turned and looked. The rifle was leaning just inside the front door, but by the time I turned around, I saw I wasn't going to need it as a sheriff's unit came into view. I still had the rifle in my hand when the vehicle stopped. The door opened, and Cal Duncan stepped from the car.

"You planning to shoot me, Jo?" He smiled.

"Not this time, Cal."

Cal and I had gone to school together in Kerrville. He had spent a lot of time outdoors, and now his face, rugged and brown with deep creases, reflected it. He looked like he was still physically fit, and I didn't doubt that he was still tough.

"I been meaning to come out since I heard you were home. Sorry I didn't make it under happier circumstances," he said as he ambled up the steps and shook my hand.

"Yeah, there's a lot of things we mean to do but never get around to."

"Got a few minutes?"

"Sure."

The front door opened, and Cate came back onto the porch with our coffee. Cal removed his hat when he saw her.

"Ma'am." He nodded.

"Cate, this is Sheriff Duncan. Cal, Cate Hammond."

Cate smiled and extended her hand to Cal.

"Can I get you a cup of coffee, Sheriff?"

"Wouldn't mind a cup, ma'am. Thank you."

As Cate left us alone on the porch, we sat down, and I rested the rifle against the porch wall.

"Nasty business out here, Jo. Got any idea what it was about?"

"Yeah, but I don't have any evidence. Probably involves a story I've been looking into."

"What kind of story?" he asked as Cate reappeared with his coffee and handed it to him.

He smiled as he said thanks again. Cate leaned against the porch railing and sipped her coffee.

"It started out as a story about illegals and mushroomed from there."

"Doesn't sound like something you'd usually be interested in."

"It isn't," I said, glancing at Cate. "Actually the story is my son's. I was helping him out with some background information."

"You think whoever came out here was looking for you, and Lena got in the way?"

"Probably, but like I said, Cal, I can't say for sure."

"No idea what they were looking for?"

"I was just beginning to research the story. Hell, I could have it right in front of me and wouldn't know what I was looking at yet, so if it involved the story, they were a little premature."

"Could be someone was trying to nip it in the bud."

"Maybe."

"By the way, Jo, Lena doesn't seem to have any relatives around here. Is there anyone you know we can contact to make the funeral arrangements?" Cal asked.

"I'll take care of it. She might have relatives somewhere, but I don't know where they'd be."

"Well, the county coroner will be ready to release the body later this afternoon."

"Have them call Sanderson's. I'll let them know to expect her."

Cal got up slowly until his full six-three frame was erect and handed his cup to Cate. "Appreciate it, ma'am. You be careful, Jo. And let me know if you think of anything I should know."

Rising from my chair, I shook his hand.

After Cal left, I located a phone book and looked up the number for Sanderson's Funeral Home, trying to imagine what kind of funeral Lena would like. It took about twenty minutes for me to discuss it with the funeral director. Since there wouldn't be many people attending, I opted for a simple graveside service. But at the last minute I asked the director if he could round up a mariachi group for the service. She would have liked that. That and a few beers. When I finally hung up the phone, Cate was nowhere in sight. I found her in the kitchen washing the cups.

"Everything arranged?" she asked.

"Yeah, day after tomorrow about two. Lena hated getting up early in the mornings." I smiled.

Cate placed the cups in the drainer and dried her hands. "Well, what do you want to tackle next?" she asked.

"You've done enough. I have to run into town in a little while to pay for the funeral. It'll be getting dark by then, so you should start gathering your stuff up and head on back to Austin."

"Why don't I go with you to the funeral home? We could grab something to eat in town."

I shrugged. "But then you go back to Austin. I don't want you out here after dark."

"I doubt whoever did this would be stupid enough to come back the next day. The police could still be crawling all over the place."

"Or they could be hanging around out there in the trees right this minute and know there's no one here but us."

She looked out the kitchen window, and I thought I saw her shiver slightly. "You're probably right, but I could just stay in Kerrville and come back out tomorrow morning. I know you won't stay in town."

"No one's going to run me out of my home," I frowned. "You should go back home though."

"You think it's not safe in Kerrville either?"

"Look, Cate, I don't know shit, okay. But I don't want to take a chance that someone else will get hurt. You might not believe this, but I don't want to have to worry about your safety."

She looked at me, and a slow smile crossed her lips. "I didn't think you still cared, Jo."

There was that old uncomfortable feeling again. Damn, how did she do that? I cleared my throat and left the kitchen. I had a sudden need for fresh air. I picked up my rifle on the way out the door and walked toward the barn, even though there wasn't anything there anymore. The county animal control people had picked up Jack late the night before. It had broken my heart to see such a beautiful animal slaughtered for no purpose. When I returned to the house, Cate was sitting on the couch looking through a manila folder.

"You about ready to go?" I asked.

"In a minute. What's this?" she asked, pointing at the folder.

I looked over her shoulder. "Just some notes about what Lena found about the meatpacking plant."

"What meatpacking plant?"

"The one over at Mountain View. Sarita told me Kyle's story about illegals was actually about the meatpacking plant hiring illegals to process their meat."

"When did you talk to Sarita?"

"She came out here a couple of days after I left San Antonio. It seems Kyle got the idea for the story from her to begin with. She asked me to continue helping him from the shadows. At first I turned her down, but Lena jumped in my shit about it. That was how she got involved. The locals over there weren't going to talk to some gringa like me, so she got herself a job in Mountain View and talked to anyone she could about the plant. These are mostly just scribbles about what she told me from those conversations. Most of it doesn't make sense, but I haven't had a chance to sit down and go over it."

"Maybe I can help you sort it out."

"Like old times?"

"But they were good times," she said, leaning back on the couch and smiling. "What do you think of Sarita?"

"Seems like a nice enough girl. Straightforward, educated. And she loves Kyle. No doubt about that. If he keeps doing what he's doing, she could be in for more than a little heartache."

Cate laughed. "Now, that sounds more like old times."

"Maybe you should warn her before she makes the same mistake."

"She wouldn't believe it. I didn't. But it wasn't all bad."

"Bad enough. Ready?"

Chapter
Fifteen

I FOLLOWED CATE into town, checking the rearview mirror more often than usual. She waited outside while I took care of my business with Sanderson's, and then we drove to a small family restaurant in town. We were seated in a booth where I could see anyone who entered. It wasn't the kind of place where illegals and thugs would hang out, and I was sure I would notice anyone who seemed out of place. I was prepared to follow Cate all the way to Austin if I had to. The sooner she was out of the picture, the better I was going to feel. We placed our order and snacked on breadsticks while we waited.

"Did you bring the folder with you?" she asked.

"Yeah. It's in the car."

"Why don't we look it over while we wait?"

After I brought the folder back inside, she took a couple of papers and glanced at them while I scanned the sheet left on top. Opening her purse, she took her glasses and a pen out to circle a few things, jotting notes to herself in the margins. I could see her mind working as she read.

"What's this?" she asked, pointing at the page.

"I don't know. I can't read upside down."

Rather than hand the paper to me, she got out of the booth and slid in next to me. Placing the paper in front of me, she pointed to three capital letters on the page: ABP.

"That's the name of the processing plant. American Beef and Pork."

"How are they involved, other than the fact that they hired illegals?"

"Everyone hires illegals, but Lena thought the number they hired was suspicious. It's one thing to get three or four, but they apparently had a few more than normal."

"How many more?"

"A couple hundred or so."

"Hmm. That does seem like a lot of people slipping through the cracks."

"Lena told me some of her relatives had worked for ABP, but they were laid off and replaced by illegals. She was still pissed at the company, which was why she was willing to do some investigating."

"But like you said, hiring illegals isn't a big deal in Texas. The company can always claim ignorance, and they don't face much, if any, monetary loss for hiring them."

"According to Sarita, the number of Hispanics in Mountain View has grown about four hundred percent in the last few years."

"How does she know that?"

"Said she used to teach in Mountain View before moving to San Antonio. She suspected most of them were illegals, but they all had papers."

"Wouldn't take a genius to fake papers."

"I talked to a worker from the plant who was laid off recently. He claimed there were a lot of false documents among the workers, but the INS doesn't have the manpower to check them all out. Plus they always seemed to know when the INS was planning a raid and called in sick."

"What's this?" she asked, pointing to the paper in front of her.

The letter C was written three or four times on that page and the next one.

"Some big shot with ABP. His name is in here somewhere," I said looking through the rest of the papers. "Like I said, I haven't had time to organize all this yet."

I finally found the page where I had jotted down a name.

"Here it is," I said. "Camarena. I'm pretty sure he's C. Everyone Lena talked to mentioned him, but I don't know what he does exactly. Lena thought he was some kind of attorney."

"Do you have his first name?"

"Felix."

Cate leaned back in the booth and closed her eyes.

"Tired?" I asked.

"A little." She opened her eyes and looked at me. She

took a deep breath and exhaled slowly. She was sitting close to me, and I could feel the warmth of her body through my shirt sleeve.

"Well, our food will be here soon. Then you can go back home and get rested up."

"I guess so. Actually, I told Susan I was taking a couple of days off to check on Kyle."

"Susan seems like a nice woman."

"She's an excellent tax attorney."

"Can't beat a woman who's good at her work, obviously wealthy, and not too bad looking. Spiffy dresser, too. Maybe you should hook up with her."

She smiled. "She's asked me to live with her."

I wasn't really surprised but wasn't sure what to say. "Congratulations."

"I haven't said yes. Things have been a little hectic lately."

"It'll settle down."

"How would you feel about that, Jo?"

The question surprised me. "Well, it's not really any of my business, now is it."

A waitress approached carrying a large tray. Cate returned to her side of the booth, and we waited while the waitress finished setting food on the table. When she was satisfied that we had everything we needed, she picked up the tray and left.

"Have you told Kyle about you and Susan?"

"He knows I'm fond of Susan, and they get along pretty well. But then, it's none of his business either."

People were fond of their dog, their comfortable old shirts, and their favorite maiden aunt; but it seemed like a strange choice of words about a woman who apparently hoped to be sharing your bed on a permanent basis, I thought with some satisfaction. I wouldn't allow myself to wonder about the extent of Cate's current relationship with Susan Bradley.

We were both hungrier than we thought, and the food disappeared quickly. As we chatted over a cup of coffee and even managed to have a few laughs, I was beginning to feel at peace again and it felt good. I had spent most of my life in dangerous situations. If I had wanted to live dangerously, I could have asked Cate to stay with me. She might have agreed, but I had decided to retire from dangerous living.

She waited while I paid for our meal, and then I walked her to her car.

"Thanks for coming down, Cate. It was a mess, wasn't it?" I smiled.

"You'll get it back in shape. I'm glad there was something I could do. I owed you for trying to help Kyle, even if it didn't turn out the way I'd hoped."

"You never know. I might still be able to help. Lena's death has made me mad. So even if he doesn't want my help, he won't have much choice. The story is his, but the revenge belongs to me."

She reached out and touched my face. "Don't do anything careless, Jo. It's already getting out of hand. I don't want to see anyone else get hurt either."

I took her hand and held it. "It's too late now. Whoever is behind this knows I'm involved, and they know Kyle is, too. They have to be flushed out before any of us can feel safe again."

I glanced down and realized I was holding her hand. I didn't want to let it go but opened my hand to release it anyway.

"You better hit the road before it gets any later. I'll follow you for a while."

"Making sure I go home." She smiled.

"Making sure no one is going with you."

She nodded and got into the car. I heard the door locks click and as soon as she started her car, I went to mine, following her for nearly thirty miles before pulling over and making a U-turn back toward the ranch.

Chapter
Sixteen

A LITTLE BEFORE two on Tuesday afternoon I pulled into the drive of Sanderson's Funeral Home. There were a few cars in the adjacent parking area. It was a bright day, and only wisps of clouds marked the blue of the sky. After slipping my jacket on, I briefly checked my appearance in the reflection in the car window.

I took a deep breath and pulled the front door open, removing my sunglasses as I entered. Funny thing about funeral homes. They're always so quiet, as if the slightest noise might awaken their customers. I caught the door to make sure it closed quietly behind me. When I turned around, the funeral director was there, the deep pile carpeting silencing his approach.

"Ms. Carlisle," he said quietly, extending his hand. "My condolences."

"Everything ready, Mr. Sanderson?" I asked.

"Yes. We'll be leaving shortly. The mariachis will meet us near the entrance to the cemetery."

"Fine," I said softly. All I wanted was for the day to end.

"Father Ramon is here. If you have a moment he'd like to speak to you."

I nodded and waited while Sanderson went to get the priest. Father Ramon looked too young to have been a priest very long. He was dark complexioned with thick black hair and intense brown eyes. He was dressed in a black suit and clerical collar.

"Ms. Carlisle," he said with no hint of an accent.

"Father," I nodded as I shook his hand.

"I was wondering if there was anything you could tell

me about Ms. Rubio? I'm afraid I didn't know her."

I had to smile. "And I'm afraid she probably never visited your church, Father. But I know she was Catholic. She was a good woman who gave her life helping a friend. She lived a hard life and did the best she could."

He looked at me and smiled warmly. "Then I shall do the best I can for her."

He turned and followed Sanderson while I slipped my sunglasses back on and left to get in my car. As I turned down the sidewalk, I was surprised to see Cate standing next to my Blazer. She was wearing aviator-style sunglasses and a black suit. A moment later I saw that she wasn't alone. Kyle and Sarita were standing on the driver's side of the car. I took keys from my pocket as I approached them, hoping that an already unpleasant day wasn't going to get worse.

"I'm very sorry about your friend, Ms. Carlisle," Sarita said sincerely as she hugged me briefly.

"Thank you, Sarita."

Kyle didn't speak, but his sullen look told me that he was there under protest.

"I'm surprised to see you here," I said in a low voice as I looked across the Blazer at Cate.

"I thought we should be. It seemed the least we could do."

"The service is going to be at the cemetery."

Cate nodded and looked at Kyle. "You and Sarita take my car. I'll ride with Jo," she said, tossing him her keys. Then she turned back to me. "If that's all right."

"Fine," I answered as I walked around the car and unlocked the passenger door.

I opened the door and waited for Cate to get in. Kyle took Sarita's hand and went to Cate's Seville. By the time I got in the car, the hearse was pulling around the corner of the building, and I started the engine and turned on my headlights. Cate unbuttoned the jacket to her suit as she adjusted her seatbelt. There was a faint white pinstripe in the suit that I hadn't noticed in the sunlight. Beneath the jacket, she wore a white, sleeveless, V-neck top that looked like a suit vest.

"A little cool today," I said, looking through the rearview mirror at Kyle and Sarita in the car behind me.

"It's early. It might still warm up," Cate said.

The hearse stopped three blocks from the cemetery

where six mariachis were waiting. Six men I didn't know waited as Sanderson opened the rear of the hearse. Father Ramon wore an embroidered white and purple robe over his suit and said a quiet prayer as the coffin was taken from the vehicle. The coffin rolled quietly from the hearse and the six strangers hoisted it onto their shoulders. As the men carrying the coffin reached the front of the hearse, the mariachis began playing. I helped Cate out of the car, and we began a short procession toward the cemetery, walking silently toward a canopied site. The whole service didn't last more than twenty or thirty minutes, and Father Ramon did a surprisingly good job of eulogizing Lena Rubio, a total stranger. Secretly, I hoped he never found out anything else about her life. Whatever religious beliefs she may have held in the past had left this world long before her soul had. When the final prayers were said, I thanked Father Ramon and gave him a donation for his church.

"I appreciate you coming, Cate," I said as we walked back toward our cars.

"Would it be all right if we followed you back to the house?"

"It's not exactly ready for company."

"I might have some information for you that will be helpful."

"What did you have to do to get him here?" I asked, glancing back at Kyle.

"If it wasn't for Sarita, he probably wouldn't be."

"Maybe we should put this reunion off for another time."

"It's already been too long, and it won't get easier as more time passes."

"Do you want to ride with me and let them follow?"

She nodded. I started my car while she went to speak to Kyle. Through the rearview mirror they appeared to be exchanging heated words. I was tempted to get out of the car, but before my thoughts got any further, I saw Cate coming back toward the Blazer.

"You were right," I said as she got in and buckled her seatbelt. "Looks like it's warming up."

Neither of us spoke again until I drove out of the city limits.

"Have you had any trouble since Saturday?"

"No. It's been pretty quiet. Cal sends a unit by a couple

of times a day. Actually had a good night's sleep last night."

"Maybe whoever was responsible believes Lena's death will convince you to drop the story."

"Then whoever 'they' are don't know me very well. I don't want to sound ungrateful or anything, Cate, but why the hell did you drag Kyle here?"

"I thought he needed to see that sometimes a story can have serious consequences. And maybe I'm hoping he'll accept your help."

"I'll give him whatever I have, but I'm not doing it for the damn story. This is personal, and I don't want him in my way."

"Then you're going to continue investigating the story?"

"To wherever and whomever it leads."

As I got out of the Blazer in front of my home, I noticed that Kyle was leaning against the door of the Seville looking around the ranch. It had been a long time since he had been here, but it hadn't changed much over the years. Cate walked back to her car and took a small bag from the backseat as I took off my jacket and waited on the porch.

"What's with the bag?" I asked as I opened the front door.

"I thought I'd change out of this suit."

She entered the house and went upstairs to the second floor. I threw my jacket over a chair in the living room and went into the kitchen for something to drink. I was pouring a glass of tea when Sarita came into the room.

"Tea?" I asked.

"I could use something to drink. Thank you." She smiled.

I took a second glass from the cabinet and poured tea into it. "There's sugar in the canister if you want it. And I think there's some lemon in the refrigerator."

"This is fine," she said as I handed her the glass. "Ms. Carlisle, I can't tell you how very sorry I was to hear about Ms. Rubio. I feel like it was my fault."

"It's no one's fault, Sarita. She wanted to help. Just didn't quite work out the way we thought it would."

We drank in awkward silence for a few minutes.

"Look, Sarita, I don't know why Kyle is here. If you and Cate think this is going to lead to some kind of instant parental bonding, you're wrong."

"I don't really know what I expect, Ms. Carlisle."

"Just Jo, please."

"Okay, Jo. You see, I love Kyle very much."

"Even a fool like me can see that," I said with a smile.

"But he's become restless and distant since he began researching this story, and I don't know how to bring him back."

I leaned against the counter and took a long drink of my tea. "I've made some monumental mistakes in my life, Sarita. I used to be consumed with my work, too, so if you're planning a life with Kyle, you should know that he won't let anything stand in the way of a story. Not even you. He's got a big story on the line now, and like a junkie looking for a fix, the next one will have to be even bigger. Although I'm sure he loves you very much, he'll love the story more. Shit." I laughed. "I started the same way. As long as the big stories keep coming, he'll keep chasing after them until, in the end, he'll leave you in his dust, sweetheart."

"Is that what you did?"

"I've been shot three times, Sarita, and with every bullet my prestige as a journalist grew. I became addicted to the thrill, the danger. I loved it," I said. "But you know what? When I got to the top and looked around, there wasn't anyone there except me. There wasn't anyone to share it with. I had a career that I loved, but I had to give up a hell of a lot to get it. I hurt a lot of people, including Cate and Kyle, along the way. You're a nice young woman. I wouldn't want to see Kyle hurt you and leave you alone the way I did Cate."

"You don't blame her for leaving you then?"

"Hell, I was surprised she waited so long."

"She must have loved you very much."

I looked at her and blinked hard. "I like to think she loved me as much as I loved her. But eventually she knew she couldn't depend on me to be there for either of them. I loved her enough to let her go."

"Maybe you didn't really know what love was."

I smiled at Sarita. "Maybe I still don't." As I raised my glass to my lips, I saw Cate standing in the kitchen doorway and wondered how long she had been there. "I see you got comfortable," I said. "Want some tea?"

"I can get it. Why don't you get out of that suit? It's nice, Jo, but it's really not you." She smiled.

"Yeah, that sounds like a good idea," I said. "Excuse me, ladies."

I went upstairs to my bedroom and peeled out of the suit. As I hung it in the closet, I wondered if I could return it to the store. Chances were good that I'd never wear the damn thing again, I thought as I slipped on a pair of jeans and a T-shirt. Taking my old desert boots from the closet, I sat down on the bed to tie them before wandering into the bathroom and splashing water on my face. As I was drying my face and hands, I looked out the bathroom window and saw Kyle walking toward the barn. I knew Cate and Sarita expected me to talk to him, to reach some kind of working arrangement about his story, but I was in alien territory. I had never really worked with anyone in my life and didn't have a clue how to go about it. What can you say to someone you haven't seen in fifteen years, someone you knew hated your guts and wished you'd never resurfaced. Maybe there wasn't anything I could say. Maybe I could give him advice on a professional level, one reporter to another. If he rejected it, too bad. He could learn to take his lumps the way I had.

I threw the towel over the shower door and went back down the stairs. A familiar smell from the kitchen stopped me as I went toward the front door to confront my past. When I looked in the kitchen, Cate and Sarita were standing at the counter, talking and laughing together like old friends.

"What are you two doing?" I asked.

"Cate told me you like enchiladas," Sarita said.

"I do indeed," I said.

"It won't be long until they're ready," Cate said.

"Well, I think I'll get some fresh air while I wait," I said, recognizing the opening she had left for me.

Leaving the house, I walked to the barn but didn't see Kyle and guessed he'd wandered off somewhere. I rested my arms on the gate in front of Jack's stall. I missed him walking up to me, waiting to run across the open pasture between the barn and the treeline, running until he lathered up and breathed heavily from the freedom and sheer exhilaration.

"I'm sorry about your friend," Kyle said, interrupting my thoughts.

"Did you look over the information she found?" I asked

without looking at him.

"It was pretty sketchy."

"Good enough for someone to get killed over," I said as I turned my head toward him. "If I find anything else you can use, I'll mail it to you."

"Your housekeeper's death is part of the story now."

"Obviously, but I'm only interested in finding whoever killed Lena, not some story. There'll always be another story, but dead is forever."

"Is that what you think? That I'm just after some story?"

"It's what I would have gone after when I was your age."

He sneered. "I'm not you."

"You're probably closer than you think, Kyle." I smiled slightly.

"You don't know shit about me," he said, his voice rising slightly. "You never bothered to hang around long enough."

"I know you got a woman in there who loves you. I wouldn't want you to shut her out and hurt her the way I did your mother."

"It's too damn late for you to be resurrected like Christ and appear in the mist giving me advice about how I should live my life."

"You're right," I said as I turned to face him. "And you're wrong. You're more like me than you think, but you don't have to make the same mistakes I did. Just make sure when you move on that you don't leave anyone behind. You'll regret it more than you can possibly begin to imagine. Believe me, I know."

Chapter
Seventeen

THERE WASN'T A lot of conversation over dinner. Cate and Sarita managed to discuss the weather, recipes, and a dozen other topics of no consequence. Occasionally, they would toss a question at Kyle or me but were generally unsuccessful at eliciting much comment.

Periodically, I would glance at Cate, and even though I tried to fight it, I couldn't help but wish I had been around to watch her grow older. There was a maturity and grace about her now that I found incredibly desirable.

The enchiladas were some of the best I'd ever eaten, and we didn't have any trouble finishing them off. It was already dark by the time we finished eating. I told Sarita to leave the dishes and I would clean them up later, but she insisted on leaving the kitchen the way she had found it. Cate made coffee, and she and I went onto the porch.

"Sarita's a good cook," I said.

"Yes, she is. She'll have to teach me how to make enchiladas like that."

"I thought you didn't care for Mexican cuisine," I said with a smile.

She laughed. "It's an acquired taste. I wouldn't want it everyday, but occasionally I just sort of crave something hot and spicy."

"Well, if hot and spicy starts to get to you, I have some antacids somewhere."

"I heard what you said to Sarita this afternoon, Jo. I hope you're wrong about Kyle."

"So do I. Sarita doesn't deserve what I did to you, Cate. Hell, no one deserves that."

"Do you think she believed you?"

"Who knows? I don't know anyone who really wants to hear the truth. I guess we all have to make our own mistakes before we learn."

"Do you ever have regrets, Jo?" she asked, turning her face toward me.

I smiled slightly without looking at her, wondering if she had an inkling of the regret I had already realized. "About a half dozen times a day, but there's not much we can do to change the past," I shrugged, raising my cup to my mouth. "It's already dead and buried."

"Does that mean you think mistakes can't be corrected?"

"If they could, I would, Cate," I said. "But I can't."

When I finally I looked at her, I didn't know what to say. There were a thousand things I wanted to say to her, but despite the fact that we had both made a living using words, when we were together, the right words never seemed to come. I didn't want her to leave. I wanted her to stay. But what would be the purpose in that? The light from inside the house was enough that I could see the profile of her face clearly. She must have sensed that I was looking at her because she turned her head toward me again and smiled.

"What are you thinking about?" she asked.

"You," I said. Realizing how sophomoric that must have sounded, I laughed. "Now there's an original line you don't hear every damn day."

Cate laughed, too, and the light caught the blue in her eyes, their effect on me unchanged by the years I'd lost. I touched the softness of her hair, pulling her toward me to kiss her forehead. She didn't seem surprised by my touch, and her eyes remained focused on my face. She leaned slightly toward me, and an impulse I had been fighting since she came back into my life surfaced as I leaned forward and kissed her. It wasn't a passionate kiss, but it was comfortable and familiar. Taking her face in my hands, I leaned toward her again, and her lips smiled as they parted to greet an old lover.

As I felt myself being drawn into everything Cate's lips were offering, I was snapped back to reality by Kyle's voice. "Making up for lost time I see."

We separated immediately, like two teenagers caught in the act by their parents.

"Sorry," I said. "We didn't hear you sneak up on us." There was irritation in my voice and Cate touched my arm.

"It's time to go, Mom. That is, if you think you can manage to break away from this romantic interlude."

"This would probably be a good time for you to shut up, son," I said.

"You don't have the right to call me son."

"You're right. And now that you've embarrassed your mother, I think you should just apologize and leave it at that."

"Or what?" he challenged.

I shook my head. I couldn't believe the incredible stupidity I was hearing. "Kid, you don't know..."

"That's enough, Jo," Cate said.

"No, it isn't, Cate. The kid has a shitload of anger inside. Unless I'm mistaken, it wasn't long ago that you told me how bad it was to keep your feelings inside. That sooner or later they were going to ooze out. Well, guess what, baby, they're oozing all over the fuckin' porch here, so butt out. I wouldn't want him to suffer any more psychological or emotional trauma than he already has because of me," I said as Sarita came onto the porch.

"Sarita, please take Kyle back into the house. We'll be leaving in a few minutes," Cate said.

Sarita stepped toward Kyle, and he cast her a glance that would have frozen water in midair.

"Come on, kid. You know you're dyin' to tell me off. What're you waitin' for? This is your big chance. Do it!" I demanded, taking a step toward him.

"Stop it, Jo. You're not mad at him. You're mad because of what happened to Lena. Don't take your anger out on your son," Cate said.

"Why don't you and Sarita go into the house and let me and 'my son' work this out?"

To my surprise, Sarita went to Cate and took her by the arm. "I think that's an excellent idea, Cate," Sarita said.

I looked at Kyle and said, "You got a keeper there, kid. Don't fuck it up the way I did and maybe you won't lose her." I went down the steps of the porch and stood on the lawn. "I'm waiting, Kyle. What's it going to be? Are you as pissed off as I am right now?"

He came down the steps as Sarita and Cate went into the house. Taking his jacket off, he threw it back toward the porch. "Stay away from my mother," he said, glaring at me.

"Shit!" I laughed. "If I could've done that to begin with, we wouldn't be here having this lovefest right now. My problem was that I couldn't stay away from her."

"Looks like you're still having a problem with that."

"In case you haven't noticed, your mother is a damned attractive woman," I said with a smile.

"She deserves better than you."

"Won't argue with that."

"Then why were you coming on to her a few minutes ago?"

"I didn't plan it. It just happened. You know, full stomach, moonlight, all that crap."

"What would you have done if I hadn't come onto the porch?"

"I don't know, and, frankly, I'm a little pissed that I won't be finding out."

Taking a deep breath, I glanced at the house where I knew Cate and Sarita were watching us. I finally decided that this verbal sparring wasn't getting us anywhere and turning toward the house, I began to walk away.

"We're not finished!" he yelled.

"You can stand there all night thinking about it if you want to, but I'm finished."

As I walked toward the steps, he grabbed my arm and spun me around. When he looked at me, I saw the hurt and anger of a child in his eyes.

"I'm sorry, Kyle," I said. "I never meant for you to be hurt. I thought I was doing the right thing and still do. Your mom did a great job raising you and she didn't need me for that."

There was an irony in the way he suddenly laughed. "What she doesn't need is you climbing back into her bed for a quick fuck."

I clenched my hands into fists, trying to restrain the rising anger I was feeling. Taking a step toward him, I said, "I don't ever want to hear you talk like that where your mother is concerned again."

"Why? Isn't that what you were doing tonight? Sniffing out a bunkmate?"

"Never crossed my mind," I said as calmly as I could.

"Bullshit! Why don't you just admit that you still want her?"

"Because I've already hurt her enough. Unless you can learn something from my mistakes, you're letting your hatred for me run your life. Right now, you're carrying around a shitload of emotional baggage and not really living your life. So why don't you get Sarita and your mother and go on home before you throw away everything you love, too."

I turned back toward the house and was halfway up the steps before he spoke again.

"She still loves you," he said bluntly. "She's always loved you even though you didn't give a shit about her."

I turned my head and looked at him without speaking and continued into the house. Sarita and Cate were standing in the middle of the living room as I passed through and climbed the stairs to the second floor. I needed to regain control of myself. Kyle was right. I did still want Cate, but he was wrong about her still loving me. I washed my face quickly before going back downstairs. Sarita had her arm around Kyle's shoulder and was whispering to him.

"Y'all drive careful now, ya hear," I said. "And thanks again for the enchiladas, Sarita."

She looked at me and smiled as she nodded.

"Take my car and find a place to stay in Kerrville for the night," Cate said to Kyle. "There's a Holiday Inn on the highway. I still need to talk to Jo for a few minutes."

Turning to me, she asked, "Will you take me to town in a little while?"

"Of course."

I was as surprised as Kyle by what she said. He frowned at her. "We can wait outside."

"No, you go ahead and get rooms for us."

"You're not planning to do anything...stupid, are you?" he asked.

"If I were it certainly wouldn't be any of your business," she replied in a cold, controlled voice.

Kyle looked at her over his shoulder as he and Sarita left the house. Cate left the living room and went into my office. When she returned, she was carrying the small bag she had brought with her.

"Before you and Kyle began your heart to heart, there was something I had to show you," she said as she removed a large envelope from her bag. "And thanks for not slapping him. I heard what he said, and I know you wanted to."

"I'm sure whatever you have there is important, but would you mind if I grabbed a cup of coffee before you tell me about it?"

"Bring me one, too."

She seemed to be absorbed in her mysterious envelope by the time I returned with our coffee.

"I could have told you about this Saturday, but I wanted to check a few things first."

"What?"

"About ABP," she said, handing me a small stack of papers. "I went to the office Saturday night as soon as I got back to Austin. I don't know how much they will help you, and I could lose my license if anyone knew I gave them to you. It does breach attorney-client privilege."

I looked through the papers for a few minutes while she drank her coffee.

"How long has ABP been a client of your firm?" I finally asked.

"They were Susan's client when I came on board. I haven't done any work for them personally, but I know she bills them for quite a few hours every month."

"She does their taxes?"

"Yes. There's a name on the last page that might interest you."

Flipping to the last page, I scanned it until I saw what she was talking about. Felix Camarena was listed as a legal consultant for ABP.

"I think I met him once when he was with Susan," she said.

"But you don't handle any of their work."

"No. I took these files from her office. Actually, they're just copies, but it still causes an ethics problem."

"You know anything about Camarena?"

"Uh-uh," she managed between sips. "If he's licensed in Texas, I can get some information about him through the Texas Bar Association though. I can check when I get back to work tomorrow afternoon."

"No, I'll check. You've already bent the rules far enough."

"If you call, ask for Carole Hutchinson. We went to law school together. Give her my name, and I'm sure she'll look up whatever you need."

I leaned back and read over the material more closely. I

don't know shit about taxes except that they're too high, so I wasn't even sure what I was reading. The next to last page was a listing of corporate expenditures. "What are miscellaneous expenditures?" I asked.

"Could be almost anything, but it's generally things that are too small on their own to merit an itemization."

"Sort of like a big carpet to sweep junk under?"

"Sort of," she said with a smile.

I slipped the papers back into the envelope and glanced at my watch. "I'll look over these again in the morning. I have a friend who does my taxes. Maybe I can get him to look at these for me. I'll remove the company's name and your firm's name before I give them to him."

"He probably won't find anything unusual. Susan's very good at what she does."

"Is it possible she's covering something up for ABP?"

"I can't believe that, Jo. Susan Bradley is one of the most respected tax attorneys in the state. If something illegal is going on, I'm sure she isn't aware of it."

"Well, don't mention any of this to her."

"Don't worry, I won't."

"Grab your bag, and I'll drive you into town before Kyle worries about you."

She stood up and took my coffee cup. "I'm too old to need a chaperone or a curfew," she said with a smile.

I followed her into the kitchen and waited while she rinsed out the cups. "I'm sorry if today didn't turn out the way you hoped it would," I said.

"All I could do was give it a try," she said as she dried her hands.

"He's built up a lot of anger. Give him more time. Once I'm out of the picture again, he'll settle down."

"I used to be angry, too, but it wasn't accomplishing anything, so I just tried to remember the good times. Unfortunately, Kyle doesn't remember you well enough to have many memories, good or bad."

"He'll be okay."

"Can I ask you something, Jo?"

"Why not?" I shrugged. "Seems to be an evening for venting frustrations."

"Do you know why I left you?"

"I presumed it was because I was an absentee parent and partner," I answered.

"When I wrote and told you I was leaving you, I never heard a word back from you. Did you think so little of us that it wasn't worth coming home for?" she asked.

"Of course not."

"Then why didn't you fight it?"

I didn't want to answer her questions, but she was backing me into a corner, forcing me to talk about things I was uncomfortable discussing, even with her. "You deserved better than you were getting from me. We both knew that. I didn't want you to be unhappy any longer."

"And you thought I'd be happier alone?"

"I thought you'd find someone else," I said. "Someone who could give you everything I couldn't. I had to make a decision, whether right or wrong, that I thought was best for all of us."

Damn, how did she always manage to make me squirm when we talked?

"You ready?" I asked, changing the subject.

"Yes," she smiled.

She walked past me toward the living room, brushing her hair back with one hand as she stopped to close her bag. I wondered if she knew she could still drive me crazy with even the smallest mannerisms. Against my better judgment, I walked up behind her, hesitating a moment before I finally put my hands on her shoulders. As she tilted her head back slightly toward me, I could smell the fragrance of her hair and closed my eyes to inhale it, sliding my hands down her arms until they encircled her. I stood there holding her, wanting to finally comfort her for everything we'd both lost even though I was a decade and a half too late. I could have held her all night. I wanted to. Crossing her arms on top of mine, she leaned against me, and I lowered my head to kiss her neck.

As she turned in my arms to face me, I let my hands slide along her waist and up her back. She looked at me and I met her lips with mine. There was something different in her kiss. It had all the passion of the twenty-five-year-old woman I had fallen in love with, but the passion was now blended with the maturity of an adult woman as her arms went around my neck and pulled me closer. When our lips parted, I held her tightly against me.

"I tried to stop loving you," I whispered. "I couldn't, but I never meant to hurt you."

She kissed my neck and rested her forehead against my shoulder as we stood with our arms around each other, afraid to make another mistake.

"Come on," I said, kissing the top of her head. "I better get you into town before it gets any later."

She nodded, and we both knew it was the right decision.

Chapter
Eighteen

WHEN I WOKE up the next morning, my eyelids fluttered as I waited for my eyes to focus on the clock next to the bed. The last time I had looked it was four-thirty. I felt like I had been sleeping for hours, but it was only seven. I wanted desperately to roll over and sleep again, but once I wake up, I'm up for the day. The worst thing about waking up early and being alone is that you're left with nothing except your own thoughts.

I had to smile as I recalled the events that had transpired the evening before. Cate and I had arrived at the Holiday Inn about ten-thirty and been greeted by Kyle in the lobby. There was a look of relief and contempt on his face, but we managed to avoid another confrontation. I was proud of him for being protective of his mother, and yet, at the same time, annoyed. He had insisted on escorting her to her room, and, as I backed out of the parking lot, I saw him on the balcony outside her room, waiting to make sure I left.

I had to wait nearly two hours before picking up the phone and calling directory assistance for the number to the Texas Bar Association in Dallas. If they opened for business at nine, perhaps I could catch someone before they got too busy. Several rings later a woman's voice announced that I had reached the Bar Association.

"Carole Hutchinson, please," I said.

The line went quiet, and for a few minutes I wondered if I had been disconnected. I was thinking about hanging up and trying again when I heard a breathless voice on the other end.

"This is Carole Hutchinson," she said.

"Good morning. My name is Joanna Carlisle, and I was

told to contact you for some information," I said.

"By whom?"

"Cathryn Hammond."

There was an immediate change in her voice. "Lord, I haven't talked to her in months. How is she?"

"Fine as far as I can tell."

"What kind of information are you looking for, Ms. Carlisle?"

"I'm a reporter, and I need some background information about an attorney whose name appears in a story I'm working on."

"Why don't you just ask the attorney? Most have a bio on hand just in case he or she decides to run for political office." She chuckled.

"I would, but he's out of the state right now, and I'm sort of facing a deadline."

"Who's the attorney?"

"Felix Camarena."

"And what exactly do you need to know about Mr. Camarena?"

"Basics. Age, birthdate, where he attended law school, awards. That sort of thing."

"Hang on, and I'll see what I can pull up on the computer."

I heard keys clicking in the background. Otherwise, there was only the sound of her breathing.

"Okay, here it is. Got a pencil?"

"Yeah."

"Felix Cesar Camarena. Born fifteen August nineteen fifty—a boomer—in San Antonio. Did an undergrad in business at Pan American and then on the UT Law. A couple of awards from Hispanic organizations after he graduated, but nothing recently."

"When did he graduate from law school?"

"'Eighty-one. Apparently he does both criminal and civil law, but he's not board-certified in a specialty."

"Any complaints listed?"

"Nothing serious. Just a couple of contempts of court."

"Okay, I appreciate the information."

"Give Catie my best when you talk to her again."

"I will, and thanks again."

Catie? I had never heard anyone call her that before. I slipped the paper with the information on it into my folder.

Pulling my wallet from my pocket, I found a piece of paper with Pauli's phone number on it and dialed again. When he answered, we got right down to business without the social amenities. He agreed to see what he could find about Felix Camarena, and I filled him in on what had happened to Lena.

"Why don't you bring everything to San Antonio, Jo? Stay with me a few days, and we'll do some deep diggin'. I got a line on Freddie Escobar. Maybe it's time to jack his ass up a little to see if anything but shit falls out."

"I can get a room, Pauli. Don't want to put you out."

"If you get in my way, I ain't afraid to throw your skinny ass out. When will you get here?"

I agreed to meet him at his house around one. Hanging up the phone, I packed a bag and grabbed my camera. This time I didn't give a damn if anyone saw me taking pictures. I wanted whoever was screwing with my family to know I was after them, and the more obvious I was, the better. Come after me, you bastards, I thought. This time attack someone more prepared to defend herself.

It was a little before one-thirty when I pulled into Pauli's driveway, and the front door opened before I got there. He was chewing the life out of the remains of yet another cigar stub as I approached. He took my bag when I reached him and threw it onto a couch as we went toward his office.

He picked up a file folder and flipped it open. "Might have something," he said as he looked over the papers in the folder.

"About Camarena?"

"Yeah, but it's a weak connection. Freddie Escobar is the grand poohbah of the Conquistadors, and they're into all kinds of dirty shit. I talked to a couple of paper pushers over at INS, and they think Escobar might be involved in smuggling illegals but haven't got enough to bust his ass yet. Course, it ain't like they're working on it full time. Plus they got all them pesky rules they gotta follow." Pauli chuckled.

"So what does that have to do with Camarena?"

"Maybe nothin'. But Mrs. Escobar's name before she met and married Mr. Escobar was Senorita Camarena. I have someone checking a few records, but it's possible that Felix and Freddie are cousins. The other thing is that when any of the Conquistadors get into trouble their attorney of preference seems to be your friend Felix Camarena, Esquire."

"Is there any record that Camarena was ever a member of the gang?"

"Not unless it's sealed in some old juvie file buried in the bowels of the legal system. But an educated guess would be that he was at some point."

"He couldn't have been in much trouble, or he'd never have gotten a license to practice law."

"If we make a few, unsubstantiated assumptions, we can figure Felix has at least some kind of family connection to the Conquistadors. He may have been a member but more like a hanger-on actin' and lookin' tougher than he was. He made it through law school, so we know he's not your typical gang moron. May have been more of a planner than a participant."

"Theoretically, this sounds good, but how can we link them together?"

"Personally, I'd talk to Escobar."

I couldn't help laughing out loud. "And you think he's going to give us Camarena?"

"No, but if I can shake his cage hard enough, he might say or do something stupid. If you're game, I know where he probably is."

"Now?"

"Unless you'd like to sit here thinkin' and waitin' for something more concrete to drop in your lap," he said. "Give me a sec to change my clothes."

In less than twenty minutes, we were careening through traffic, heading deep into the underside of San Antonio. Pauli slowed down as we reached a business area that could have been beamed up from Mexico City. None of the businesses had signs in English, but I managed to figure out what a few of them were by looking at their window displays. Pauli looked relaxed, and there was a grin on his face.

"I hope you know where the hell you're going."

"Old stompin' grounds."

"I thought you were in vice?"

"You think Mexicans don't have vice? Just look around, for Christ's sake."

The street offered a strange mixture of people. A

Mexican grocery on one corner displayed a variety of fruits and vegetables in bins in front of the store, while across the street on the other corner, a group of four or five women displayed a variety of enticements intended to satisfy your libido instead of your stomach. Sedate looking family vehicles mingled with garish lowriders.

"Interesting place," I said.

"How about some food?" Pauli pulled to the curb in front of a restaurant with a colorful, handpainted sign announcing we were at Consuela's. After looking around, he pointed to a bright yellow lowrider in front of us and said, "Looks like we're here right on time."

"For what?"

"A little lunch and a little conversation with Freddie Escobar."

The interior of the restaurant appeared to be clean and was divided into two sections — one for eating and one for drinking. From a quick glance around, it appeared that the two functions mingled easily with one another. Two or three couples sat with huge platters in front of them. Enchiladas, quesidillos, and tamales were accompanied by generous helpings of refried beans and Spanish rice. Pitchers of beers sat in the middle of each table. A well-preserved woman who looked to be in her late sixties was talking to one of the couples. As I watched the restaurant customers eat, I decided there was something about Mexican food that invited huge bites, barely leaving room for the jaws to move up and down. The food smelled inviting, but I knew Pauli had no intention of dining.

The second room contained a long, shiny bar, and a few of the drinkers also had platters in front of them. Pauli moved toward the bar area and stopped in the doorway; his huge frame made it impossible for anyone to get past him as he scanned the room and spotted what he was looking for. Looking over his shoulder, he motioned for me to follow him. A line of six red vinyl booths lined the wall on the far side of the bar. As we approached, I saw two men seated at one of the booths drinking beer. One of the men was young, in his twenties. His black hair was slicked back, and he was wearing a suit that would have made a pimp proud. He was laughing at something the other man had said. The second man was older, probably in his late forties, and almost distinguished-looking as a result of graying temples. He was wearing a simple tan sport shirt over loose-fitting brown gabardine slacks. When he smiled, his teeth were white and perfect beneath a full, trimmed mustache. He smiled at us, but his eyes told me he wasn't happy.

"Pauli! What a pleasant surprise," the older man said without genuine friendliness.

"Tell the pimp here to take a hike, Freddie. We got business to discuss," Pauli said without taking his eyes off Escobar.

The younger man stood up quickly and opened his mouth to speak but was silenced by a slight movement of Escobar's hand.

"We will finish this later, Ernesto," Escobar said with a fatherly smile.

When the younger man left, Pauli slid into the booth opposite Escobar. It was a tight fit. Escobar's eyes drifted from Pauli to me.

"And who is your friend?" Escobar asked.

"Just a friend," Pauli answered.

Pauli took up so much space in the booth that I decided to pull a chair over and sit at the end, straddling the table's center leg.

"What is this business we have to discuss, Pauli?"

"I'm looking for some information."

"You know me, Pauli, I will help you if I can."

"Yeah, you've always been very cooperative with the police. Real solid citizen."

"You're not the police anymore." Escobar smiled. "But ask anyway."

"Tell me about Felix Camarena."

I was surprised that Pauli had been so forthright in mentioning Camarena's name but tried not to let it show on my face.

"You have me at a loss. I don't know anyone named Felix Camarena."

"That's bullshit, Freddie. I know he's your cousin."

"You must have gotten some bad information from one of your junky snitches."

"I think Consuela should know the names of her own nieces and nephews. I just talked to her on the way in."

Escobar took a long drink from his bottle. I knew he was debating whether to believe Pauli or not.

"So he's my cousin, what of it?" Escobar said, setting

the bottle back on the table and crossing his arms in front of him.

"You seen him lately?"

"No, but I can give you the address for his office if you like."

"Your gang's still running things around here, I see," Pauli said as he shifted in the booth.

Freddie Escobar smiled. "We got no gangs here. Just concerned citizens looking out for one another."

Pauli smiled back at him. "I have to admit, Freddie, you're looking pretty upstanding these days, not like ten or so years ago."

"Everyone grows up."

"I hear you've found a nice little side business for yourself. Still bringing produce up from the Valley?"

"Uh-huh."

"Bet there's plenty of wet lettuce in those trucks, too."

"Wet lettuce would go bad before it reached San Antonio. Nothin' wet gets in my trucks."

"How far north do you carry produce, Freddie?"

"However far it needs to go. Why?"

"Just wonderin'," Pauli answered as he began sliding out of the booth. "You want me to send Ernesto back in on my way out?"

Escobar shrugged and tilted his bottle toward his mouth. Pauli hoisted himself up, and we started toward the door.

"Hey, Pauli!" Escobar called out when we were halfway across the room.

Pauli turned around and waited.

"I coulda had you and your friend killed like that," he said, snapping his fingers.

Pauli smiled and pulled a hand out of his jacket pocket, holding out a snub-nose .38 for Escobar to see. "And I coulda killed you by sneezin'."

Pauli dropped the gun back into his pocket, and we left the restaurant. He checked the rearview mirror several times until we reached a better part of San Antonio.

"Well, you got an answer about how Camarena and Escobar are tied together. Family."

"What did you have planned if he hadn't fallen for that bit about his mother?"

"Didn't have another plan. He's probably chewin' out

the old lady right now and feelin' like a dope. He looks good and talks a good game, but he's basically a muscle man. Whoever's behind this illegal thing, you can bet your ass it ain't Freddie Escobar."

That night we compiled what we had, and there still wasn't anything that would directly connect Camarena to anything illegal. I gave the pictures I had taken at Mountain View to Pauli and asked him to run the plates on the two vehicles through DMV, although I was fairly certain that at least one of them belonged to Felix Camarena.

I decided to leave the next morning and drive to Austin. There might be someone at the law school who would remember Camarena, although I didn't have a clue what I was looking for. I wanted to see Cate again, and Camarena was going to be my excuse for seeing her. I thought about calling Sarita but decided against it. Kyle would probably be at home, and I didn't want to cause any problems between them. Pauli planned to keep an eye on the Produce Terminal Market to see if anything interesting got off the trucks besides cantaloupes and lettuce.

Chapter
Nineteen

I LEFT EARLY the next morning in an attempt to avoid the traffic but was only successful until I reached Austin. Traffic periodically came to a complete stop on Interstate 35, with cars lined up on every on- and off-ramp. As I inhaled early-morning exhaust fumes, I wondered if there was ever a time when Austin traffic could be avoided. As I crossed the bridge at Town Lake, I could see the Capitol Building and knew I would be exiting the highway soon. I reminded myself that patience is a virtue even when all you can see in the rearview mirror is the grill of the tractor-trailer kissing your bumper.

Driving conditions improved only slightly after I left the interstate and made my way toward the University of Texas campus. I stopped several people to ask directions to the law school, but apparently orienteering wasn't part of the university curriculum. Most of them knew UT had a law school even if they didn't know where it was. I finally flagged down a campus cop who offered to lead me to the correct building.

The law school is located in Townes Hall, a multiple-story building located on the far side of the campus, at Twenty-Sixth and East Campus Drive. UT is built smack in the middle of the city, and apparently no one thought Austin would grow to its current size. As a result, the university didn't have the physical space to grow out. Instead it grew up. Virtually every building has multiple stories that have to accommodate the more than fifty thousand students who cram themselves into the classrooms on a daily basis. Out of necessity more than anything else, most students had abandoned any hope of driving to classes, and there were thousands of bicycles and mopeds on the campus.

I felt out of place among the students and tried for a professorial look as I entered the main doors of the law school. I looked around but didn't see a receptionist. Instead, a large sign hanging in the main hallway contained a listing of offices, and I decided that Admissions would be as good a place to start as any. Admissions was on the first floor, and after wandering through a number of corridors, I located the office. A young man behind a desk looked up when I entered.

"Excuse me," I said. "But I'm looking for some information about a graduate of the law school."

"Try Records," he said. "Second Floor on your left."

There was a staircase nearby, and I opted to take the stairs instead of the elevator. This time I found the office I was looking for immediately and felt I was making progress. I explained to a young woman what I was looking for and she frowned.

"When did you say the person graduated?"

"Nineteen eighty-one."

"You might want to try the Law School Alumni Association," she said.

Beginning to feel like a rat in a maze, I asked, "Why don't you give them a call and ask them if that's where I need to be?"

She picked up the phone and spoke to someone for a minute before hanging up. She looked at me and smiled. "That's where you need to go. The Alumni Association, but it's not in this building."

"Do you have a map?"

She dug through a couple of desk drawers. Finally, she dragged out a college catalog. Opening it to the front page, she ripped out a page containing a small map. I followed her finger as it moved across the map.

The offices of the Alumni Association were in a small single-story building a few blocks from the law school. There was a homey look about the place, and for the first time that day, I didn't feel intimidated about entering a building. An older woman was typing on a computer keyboard when I entered and explained, again, what I was looking for.

"That's a long time ago. I'm not exactly sure what we'd

have that could help you."

"I just need some background information. Mr. Camarena is mentioned in a story I'm working on, and I'm trying to find out as much as I can about him. I already have the basic stuff but would like to find something to make it more personal. Would there be anyone here who might have gone to school with Mr. Camarena, or perhaps a teacher who would remember him?"

"After twenty years, it would have to be a very old teacher. Just a minute," she finally said, getting up from her desk. She walked down a short hallway and into an office. A few minutes later she stuck her head out of the doorway and motioned for me to join her outside the office.

"You can try talking to Professor Evans. He's been here longer than anyone I know. He might remember something, but his mind isn't always as sharp as it used to be. You know how it is," she whispered.

"Yes, I do," I whispered back even though I didn't have a clue how it was.

As I followed her into the office, I saw a distinguished-looking man in his eighties sitting behind a huge walnut desk sucking on an unlit pipe.

"Professor Evans? This is the woman who wanted information about one of our graduates." Turning to me she said, "I'm sorry, but I didn't get your name."

"Joanna Carlisle."

She turned back to the old man. "This is Ms. Carlisle."

The old man pushed himself halfway out of his chair and extended a liver-spotted hand. I was afraid to grasp it too tightly for fear of crushing what remained of the bones beneath the skin.

"Thank you, Sarah," he said in a pleasant voice as he sat down again. He took the pipe from his mouth and smiled at me. It was more of a half smile as only one side of his mouth had moved, leading me to suspect that he might have had a stroke at some point.

"I appreciate you taking time to speak to me, Professor Evans," I began.

"There aren't a lot of demands on my time anymore, young lady. They only give me this office so I'll feel useful, but they don't think I know that," he said with a twinkle in his milky blue eyes.

I liked him immediately. If he knew anything I was

certain he would tell me. He was too old to keep secrets or to care who found out about them.

"Who was it you wanted to know about?"

"Felix Camarena. He graduated from the law school in nineteen eighty-one."

"Not long before I quit teaching full time. Do you have a picture?"

"No, I'm sorry, I don't."

"No matter," he said swiveling around in his chair. He pushed a button on the intercom and waited until a voice responded. "This is Cedric Evans. Would you bring a copy of the nineteen eighty-one law school annual to my office, please?"

He released the button and leaned back in his chair, still sucking on the pipe.

"Would you like a light for that, Professor?" I asked.

"Yes, I would, but the law says no smoking in public buildings."

"At your age, do you really care?" I smiled.

He laughed. "Not really, but the law is the law, and since I've spent a lifetime dedicated to teaching the glories of the law, I don't believe I'll start breaking them now. What is it you do for a living, Ms. Carlisle?"

"I'm a photojournalist. Or I was. I'm sort of retired now."

"And yet you're working on a story."

"Just helping out a younger reporter with less experience."

"Ah! So you're a teacher, too," he said with another smile. "You know, no one wants to teach anymore. No monetary reward in it, really. But what most people today don't realize is that as we get older, we all teach everyday. The young have a lot to learn if they only remember to listen."

"Some people are better at it than others."

"Even a thug on the street teaches. No one is born a thug. They learn it as they grow up—from older thugs."

A knock at the door interrupted our conversation. A young woman entered the office and handed a volume to Evans. He thanked her and flipped through the pages until he found what he was looking for, his eyebrows knitting into a frown as he closed the book.

"What do you want to know?" he asked.

"Do you remember him?"

"Very well. There are some students you never forget."

"What made him so memorable?"

"He was an extremely poor student. Had to repeat my course in torts, as a matter of fact."

"But he did manage to graduate."

"Yes, eventually. I don't know what he's doing today, but I can't imagine that he'd be more than a mediocre attorney at best."

"He's a legal counsel for American Beef and Pork."

He raised his eyebrows slightly. "I'm surprised to hear that."

"Do you know anything about him that might have taken place outside the classroom?"

"Well, I know he didn't have any money. At least not at first. I believe he worked for one of the fraternities. Doing cleanup, that sort of thing. In fact, I seem to remember seeing him at a couple of parties where faculty were invited."

"He didn't belong to the fraternity?"

"No. And I doubt they would have let him in even if he could have afforded it. During that time period, they wouldn't have pledged a Hispanic student. He was abrasive and always seemed out of place. As a matter of fact, after he failed my class, I checked his admissions papers thinking there had been a mistake made in admitting him."

"But there wasn't?"

He shook his head. "He made the lowest acceptable score on his entrance exam, so I'm sure he was an affirmative action admission. I love the law, Ms. Carlisle, but I had to disagree with the courts on that one."

"Is there anything else you can think of about him?"

"Not really. At least not anything that I know for a fact. There were some rumors after that girl died though."

"What girl?"

"I don't remember her name, but I think she dated a member of one of the fraternities. When she was murdered, the police questioned everyone at the fraternity party she had attended as well as the hired help. I believe Felix worked that party, so he must have been questioned about it."

"Do you remember the year it happened?"

"Lord, no. Probably in the late seventies or early

eighties though."

"Did the police arrest anyone?"

"They finally chalked it up as a random killing."

"Was she killed at the fraternity house?"

"I believe they found her downtown someplace, but I really can't remember the details."

"Did the police suspect someone at the fraternity house?" I asked, becoming intrigued by the story even though it wasn't what I was looking for.

"I'm afraid you'd have to ask the police about that."

"I appreciate your time, Professor Evans. You've been very helpful," I said as I stood up.

Evans seemed to be in a trance of some kind.

"Professor Evans? Are you all right?"

"What? Yes, I'm fine. You know, something a little unusual did happen involving Mr. Camarena. I didn't remember it until a few minutes ago, but it was around that same time that he began receiving financial assistance to complete school."

"What kind of assistance?"

"A private grant of some kind. I presumed it was from a Hispanic organization eager to support minority students."

"Is there any place that would have a record of the grant?"

"I'm not sure, but I'd be glad to see what I can find out if you think it's important. It would give me something to do today besides sit here and suck on this damn pipe."

When I shook his hand before leaving, his grip felt stronger. I made a mental note to keep busy until I croaked.

Chapter
Twenty

BY THE TIME I reached my car, it was ten forty-five. If I didn't get lost again, I still had time to swing by the American-Statesman. I would contact Pauli later to see what he could find out about a murder that was more than twenty years old by now. Mentally I figured it must have happened around the same time I met Cate or while I was out of the country, because it didn't ring any bells. Of course, I had been totally absorbed by Cate then and wouldn't have been paying much attention to anything else when we were together.

After twenty-plus years, there weren't any active files on old unsolved murders, but the clerk in the newspaper morgue handed me five or six spools of microfilm covering 1978 through 1982 and pointed me to a machine to look for stories covering the case. I was midway through 1980 before I looked at my watch. Twelve fifteen. I hoped Cate would be able to take a late lunch. I hadn't called to tell her I was in town, so she had no reason to expect me even though I was anxious to see her again.

Microfilm for late 1980 ran past my eyes as I quickly scanned the headlines on each page. There was no way to tell how important the newspaper had thought a dead coed was, so the story could have been anywhere, except possibly the society or sports pages. My eyes were getting tired, and I was near the end of the spool when a thirty-six-point headline sped past me. I rewound the film and read quickly over the story. The body of a UT coed, Julianne McCaffrey, had been found by someone taking a shortcut through an alleyway near Sixth Street early on the morning of November 9, 1980. She had been raped and strangled. Police believed her body had been dumped in the alley. Julianne McCaffey was a member of the Tri-Delta sorority, and the evening before her body was found, she had attended a bash at the Kappa Alpha house, according to her roommate. A picture accompanying the article showed a beautiful blonde young woman of around twenty. From the stories I had heard, every Tri-Delt was beauty queen material, and she seemed to fit that image. The police had no suspects in the case but were questioning the members of the Kappa Alpha fraternity.

A small obituary the following day listed her parents as Mr. and Mrs. Albert McCaffrey of Houston. I made a copy of the article and the obituary, paid the clerk, and made a dash for my car again. Noontime traffic was horrendous, as usual, but I was becoming accustomed to it by this point. The only advantage I had on this trip was that I had already been to Cate's office once before and wasn't totally lost. Then God must have decided to smile on me because I found a parking space in front of the Travis Professional Building. Twelve-forty-five. Not bad timing.

Peggy was sitting behind the reception desk as I burst through the glass doors of Bradley and Hammond. The look on her face indicated that she remembered me.

"Ms. Hammond, please," I said as pleasantly as possible.

Without speaking to me, she punched buttons on the phone.

"Ms. Hammond. Ms. Carlisle is at the reception desk. Do you have a few minutes?" She listened and hung up. "Ms. Hammond will meet you in the conference room. It's down this hall, last door on the left."

I thanked Peggy and tried to straighten my clothes as I walked down the hall. The thought of seeing Cate again brought a smile to my face, which was quickly erased when I opened the conference room door. She wasn't alone. The woman who had stuck her head into Cate's office during our argument a few weeks before was sitting at a large oak library table, with short stacks of law books in a semicircle in front of her. Cate was leaning over her shoulder, her hand resting easily on the woman's shoulder, and they appeared to be reading a passage from one of the books.

Cate looked up and smiled when she saw me in the doorway. "Come in, Jo. We'll be through here in just a second." Turning back to the woman, she said, "The statute is fairly ambiguous, Susan. You should be able to bend it far enough to satisfy your client."

"I know, but I'd like to find something a little stronger."

"You should have hired that law clerk we interviewed a couple of weeks ago," Cate said. "It would have saved you a lot of hours looking all this up yourself."

The woman smiled up at her. "But they're all billable hours."

The smile remained stuck on her face as she looked in my direction. Cate must have realized that we hadn't been formally introduced.

"Susan, this is Joanna Carlisle. Jo, Susan Bradley, senior partner."

I crossed the room toward her, and we shook hands. So this was my adversary for Cate's affections. She certainly had me outdressed. There didn't appear to be a wrinkle in her long-sleeve silk designer blouse, and every hair on her head was in the right place.

"Why don't we go into my office?" Cate asked. "Please excuse us, Susan."

Susan nodded and dove back into her book of statutes, whatever those might have been. I followed Cate out of the conference room and down a longer hallway that led to her office. On the way, we passed a partially open office door with Susan's name on it. Cate opened her office door and walked straight to her desk, sitting down in a comfortable-looking chair that I hadn't noticed before.

"God, I hate research!" she said.

"Then you'd make a lousy reporter."

"When did you get in town?"

"This morning. Just doing a little research," I answered with a smile.

"About Kyle's story?"

"It's becoming more interesting by the day. I can see why he'd want to go after it, and he doesn't know half of what I know."

"Can you tell me about it?"

"I thought I might do that over lunch unless you've already eaten."

"We've been buried in law books all morning. I am a little hungry."

"You might want to take a little longer than an hour.

It'll take me a while to catch you up on the story. Right now it's mostly bits and pieces, and I thought you'd be able to see an angle I hadn't found yet."

"I doubt it, Jo. You're closer to it than I am."

"You know what they say about the forest and the trees."

"Just let me tell Susan I'm leaving," she said as she got up and pulled a small handbag from a desk drawer.

I walked with her toward the conference room. As we passed Susan's office, the door was open all the way, and Susan was parked behind her desk writing on a legal pad. When Cate saw her, she stopped and tapped at her door.

"I'm going to lunch, Susan. Can I bring you back something?"

"No, thanks, I'm fine. Can you spare one more minute before you leave?"

Cate looked at me, and I shrugged. I wasn't being nosy, but I walked into Susan's office behind Cate and leaned against the doorframe to wait for what I was sure would be longer than a minute. Susan's office lacked the little feminine details of Cate's office. No plants, no color-coordinated furniture. The carpeting throughout the offices was the same, but her office was almost Spartan compared to Cate's. There were a number of prints and family pictures hanging on the walls of Cate's office, while Susan seemed to be more into official-looking documents, matted to make them look bigger than they actually were. Out of boredom more than anything else, I glanced at a few of the plaques and framed documents. There was a diploma from the University of Oklahoma granting her a degree in business administration in 1978. Under that was a larger, more ornate sheepskin announcing that she was a graduate of the University of Texas Law School. Texas-OU football weekend must be a real dilemma for good old Susan, I thought. To either side of her diplomas were citations for editing the law review and a Certificate of Recognition for her service as President of Delta Delta Delta Sorority while at Oklahoma. Glancing back at her law school diploma, I searched for a date. Graduated June 1981.

While I was absorbed in processing what I had just read, Cate tapped me on the shoulder. "Ready?" she asked.

"Yeah, sure," I smiled. "Uh, listen, maybe Susan would like to join us. Get away from the books for a while, you know. Clear her head."

"Would you care to join us, Susan?" Cate asked.

"No, I don't think so, but thanks for asking," she replied.

"Come on, Susan," I said as I slipped my arm around Cate's waist. "All work and no play makes for a dull woman."

It was the dumbest remark I could ever remember uttering, and Cate looked at me like I had gone completely around the bend. But I now wanted desperately to get Susan involved in a conversation. I was hoping that my arm around Cate would show her she didn't have a clear field to Cate's affections and drive her to protect something I knew she wanted. She looked at me for a moment, and I saw her territorial instincts kick into gear.

"Maybe I could use some time away from this," she finally said with a smile.

"Great!" I said. "Where do you two suggest? I'm not up on the good Austin restaurants anymore."

Susan looked at Cate and then back at me. "How about the Eighth Street Bar and Grill? It's not very far from here, and we haven't been there for a while."

She wasn't speaking to me but was letting me know I had trespassed into an area where she had staked a claim. If Cate was aware of any of this crap, she didn't let on.

"Would you like to go in my car?" Susan offered.

"Why don't we follow you? You know where you're going, and after lunch I need to speak to Cate alone," I said. "Unless that's a problem, Susan."

"Of course not, Jo. I'll get my car from the parking garage and meet you out front."

I opened the door of my car and waited for Cate to get settled before I went to the driver's side. I started the engine and turned on the air. I was preoccupied with my own thoughts when I heard Cate say, "There she is."

I watched as a familiar looking blue-gray Mercedes 380 SL nosed into the street and waited as several cars went by before pulling out of the garage exit. There was no doubt in my mind that this was the second vehicle I had photographed at the ABP plant.

"Nice car," I said.

"Too small," Cate replied. "You can fall into it, but it takes an ejector seat to get out gracefully if you're dressed for an evening out."

"I'll bet there's not a lot of room to maneuver in the backseat either," I said with a chuckle.

"I wouldn't know." She laughed. "It's been a long time since I spent much time in the backseat of a car."

Susan swung into a parking space in the alleyway next to the Eighth Street Bar and Grill. It had a French café look about it. Round, linen-covered tables behind a wrought iron fence lined the wide sidewalk on either side of the main entrance. It was after one, and most of the tables were already in partial shade. We found a table close to the building and sat down. A bored-looking young man approached us with glasses of water and menus. We all selected something light that wouldn't take long to prepare.

While we waited, Susan unbuttoned her jacket and leaned back, sipping her water. She frequently looked at Cate, and I would have sworn she winked at her. Cate looked uncomfortable sitting between us, and I was sorry that I had put her in that situation.

"Cate told me what happened to your housekeeper, Jo. Terrible thing."

"Yes, it was. She was a fine woman and a good friend. When I find out who was responsible, I might not be able to wait for the criminal justice system to hash it all out."

"But those things are better left in the hands of professionals, don't you agree?"

"I am a professional."

"Not a professional detective though."

"You'd be amazed what a good reporter can uncover, Susan. There are things I can find out and places I can go where the police wouldn't be welcome."

"And people actually talk to you?"

"Tell me things they wouldn't tell their own priest. Surprisingly, twenty bucks can buy a lot of information, as long as whomever you're talking to needs a fix bad enough."

"As an attorney I can tell you that kind of evidence wouldn't be considered very reliable in court."

"I'm not interested in going to court, Susan."

"Ah, yes, revenge. I forgot," she said as she wrapped both hands around her water glass and held it in front of her face.

"If revenge means justice is served, then I'm for it. A lot

of cases are never solved because the cops don't have a vested interest in digging deep enough. They're in a hurry to clear as many cases as they can. I, on the other hand, have all the time in the world, and I'm extremely patient in tracking down even minor leads."

"Still, you must admit that some cases are unsolvable."

I shook my head. "For every crime, there's someone somewhere who knows something. Hell, they might not even know they know it. For example, I was just reading about an old case that happened a couple of blocks from here."

"Really," Cate said. It was the first time she had spoken since we sat down.

"Yeah. Some sorority girl whose body was found in an alley behind Sixth Street. Raped, murdered, and dumped. I was drawn to it because it happened not long after you and I met. Back in November of nineteen eighty."

"And the case has never been solved?" Susan asked. "I'd think that proved my point, Jo. A twenty-five-year-old murder case. Whoever did it could be on another continent or dead by now."

"Or he or she could be living within spitting distance of the crime scene."

"This is beginning to sound like one of those debate cases we argued in law school," Cate said.

"Personally, I think it's a snipe hunt," Susan said over the top of her glass.

"Maybe," I said with a smile. "But I'll bet the boys at Kappa Alpha really sweated for a while."

"Kappa Alpha?" Cate said.

"She went to a party there the night she died. She was a Tri-Delt."

"Wasn't Tri-Delt your sorority, Susan?" Cate asked.

"When I was at Oklahoma," she answered, putting emphasis on the Oklahoma part as if to distance herself from the crime.

When our food arrived, Susan seemed relieved to have some other way to occupy herself. I was halfway through my sandwich before stopping to speak again.

"By the way, Cate, we've dug up a couple of interesting things for the illegals story," I said.

She looked quickly at Susan and back to me without speaking.

"We've been tracking someone who might be involved in bringing them in. A guy named Camarena who works for American Beef and Pork. Seems this Camarena has a cousin, Escobar, who might be bringing illegals in for him. It's not all tied together yet, but it shouldn't be long."

"Is this the story Kyle was working on?" Susan asked, wiping her mouth with a napkin.

"Yes," I answered. "I suspect that either Camarena or Escobar might have been involved in the murder of my housekeeper."

"It sounds like you have a lot of mights and maybes."

"It's just a matter of getting lucky and tying it all together."

I couldn't tell from Susan's demeanor whether what I said had rattled her. If she knew anything incriminating, she certainly wasn't going to tell me about it. And she didn't know where I had gotten the information about Camarena or ABP. To a total stranger, there was nothing unusual about Cate's demeanor either, but her eyes were saying volumes to me. I hoped Susan didn't know those eyes as well as I did.

Susan finished her lunch, and, shortly afterward, excused herself, saying she needed to get back to work on the case at the office. I wouldn't let her pay for her food, and we parted with a handshake. On her way out, she whispered something to Cate and gave her a quick kiss on the cheek, undoubtedly for my benefit. I smiled as she left, but a swift kick to the shin from under the table abruptly interrupted my smile.

"What was that shit all about?" Cate demanded.

"Which shit?" I asked, rubbing my shin.

"That stuff about a murdered sorority girl and Camarena. It sounded like you were interrogating Susan."

"No, I wasn't. But I've run into too many coincidences in the last few days. Just thought I'd see what kind of reaction I'd get from good old Susan."

"Surely you didn't expect her to divulge any information about ABP or Felix Camarena to you. They are her clients, and she doesn't owe you any explanation about them."

"She doesn't know where I found out about them either. I haven't given away your midnight file search."

"What could you possibly have hoped to accomplish with that conversation, Jo?"

"Truthfully, I'm hoping that she'll contact Camarena, and he'll come after me to find out what I know. Of course, if Susan is totally in the dark about what Camarena is doing at ABP, I don't have anything to worry about."

I spent another half-hour telling her what I had found out about Camarena from Professor Evans and Freddie Escobar. Although she was mildly impressed with the information, she defended Susan to the bitter end. I had tried to shake her up and had come up with squat, not even rapid blinking or a hard swallow. Cate had always been an excellent judge of character and not easily snowed by a polished demeanor. She trusted Susan implicitly, and I hoped, for her sake, that she was right.

I paid the bill and drove her back to her office. My Godsent parking place was long gone, forcing me into a few trips around the block before I spotted a car pulling away from the curb a block from her building.

"How long are you going to be in Austin?"

"Going back to San Antonio in a couple of hours. There's not much more to find here, and I need to check in with Pauli."

"Have you spoken to Kyle about what you've found yet?"

"No. I'd like to keep it as far from him as possible until it's actually time for the story to break. I might call Sarita tomorrow though. If it looks like he's stuck and just spinning his wheels, maybe whoever was responsible for having him shot will lay off. No sense going after him if he doesn't know anything."

"They might decide you're a better target."

"I've made copies of everything I've found. Pauli will have them. If something does happen, he'll give them to Kyle. He'll have to decide if the story's worth pursuing after that."

"Damn, Jo, I didn't involve you in this so you could become a sacrificial lamb."

I reached across the car and touched the tips of her hair. "I know," I said. "But considering how little I've given him, this doesn't seem like much."

Her eyes glistened. "I hate this. I wish you would chuck the whole thing."

"It's too late for that now, darlin'." I opened my door and went to the passenger side to help Cate out of the car.

"Promise me you'll be careful, Jo. Stay in San Antonio with your friend."

"If you'd ever heard the way he snores, you wouldn't ask me to do that."

"I want you to promise anyway. And look me in the eyes when you do, so I'll know you're not lying."

She knew me too well, and she knew the power her eyes had over me. I promised to stay with Pauli as I walked her to the entrance of her building and gave her his address and phone number in case she needed to contact me.

Chapter
Twenty-One

I SPENT A sleepless night in Pauli's spare bedroom, and it wasn't just that his snoring shook the wall between our rooms. All the little pieces of information I had gathered were floating around inside my head looking for a way to connect with one another. On my way out of Austin, I had stopped back at the Alumni Association and spent a little more time with Cedric Evans. He may have been older than dirt, but the man knew how to find information. He had dug back in the filed student records and come up with Felix Camarena's financial benefactor, a small company called Pan American Investments, which listed its headquarters in Kimball, Texas, a suburb of Houston. According to Professor Evans, Pan American Investments had gone belly up in the mid-eighties.

I gave up on sleep and felt my way down the dark hallway into the living room. At four in the morning, I was parked in Pauli's kitchen going over my notes again and waiting for his coffee maker to finish spitting and burping out its contents. In an effort to kill time, I began making lists of people to call and places to look on one sheet of paper. On a second sheet, I compiled a longer list of questions. Was there a connection besides business between Susan Bradley and Camarena? Had Susan known Camarena at UT Law? Was Camarena responsible for the death of Julianne McCaffrey? Even if he was, what did that have to do with the illegals story? Or with Susan Bradley for that matter? Maybe in my zeal to track the original story I had allowed myself to become sidetracked, and there were actually two stories in front of me linked only by coincidence. I made outlines, drew mind webs, anything to put all the pieces together, and was getting nowhere fast.

Around five thirty, I heard Pauli padding down the hallway. He was bleary-eyed as he came into the kitchen, barely acknowledging my presence as he headed straight for the coffee maker. Bringing his cup to the table, he eased down on a chair and looked at the papers in front of me. "Drives you nuts, don't it?"

"There's so much and yet so little here," I said, throwing my pencil down in frustration. "How did you do it for so long?"

"You were a fuckin' reporter, how did you?"

"My job was to go where they told me and shoot pictures. I didn't have to investigate the backgrounds of everyone involved."

"You never know where the next big piece of the puzzle will come from, so you just have to keep pokin' around until it turns up."

"What if it never turns up?"

"Then you're fucked and move on to the next case." He shrugged. "It happens."

"Do you have a plan for today?"

"I plan to sit here all day doin' grunt work — phone calls, that sort of thing. Gimme that list." He read over the things I had written down. "How's about I take the Pan American Investment Company and the Austin PD. You can call Mr. or Mrs. McCaffrey."

"Thanks for nothin'. I guess you haven't found out anything more about the illegals Escobar is bringing in."

"Remember Mercado? The dumb shit told me he heard there were some comin' in this week, but he was really flyin' when he told me, so who knows. To make that one you'd have to see them come in the front door illegal and go out the back door semi-legal. Then, if we could follow them to their final destination, at least we'd see the whole route. And that's only if you believe Mercado's hallucinations and want to sit on your ass for God knows how many days and nights to wait for the big arrival."

"Do we have another choice?"

"Nope. We're down to the most borin' part for now."

Less than an hour later, I found myself sipping coffee from the plastic lid of a Thermos bottle across the street from the San Antonio Produce Terminal. Pauli had insisted that I bring my camera and any telephoto lenses I had, the bigger the better. Now the camera rested on the car seat between us, equipped with a 500-millimeter lens that would have taken a picture of a gnat's ass on a grape from where we were parked. Lack of sleep, coupled with extreme boredom, began to overcome the gallon of coffee I had already consumed, and periodically, I dozed off, slouching down in the seat. Every time I got comfortable, Pauli punched me to get a shot of something. The chances were the person in question had absolutely nothing to do with anything, but Pauli planned to run them all past his buddies at the police department anyway.

By nine that morning, the Produce Terminal was bursting at the seams with restaurant owners looking for a deal on fresh produce. The Terminal was a huge open warehouse with half a dozen oversized garage doors that had to be hoisted open with chains. Samples of fruit and vegetables were displayed everywhere. Customers told each vendor what they wanted, and it appeared from the backs of trucks, which had been backed into makeshift stalls throughout the building. Seemingly it was not an efficient way to do business, but the San Antonio Produce Terminal had been operating the same way for decades. The really big produce buyers, primarily grocery chains, picked up the produce themselves in their own trucks. The Terminal wasn't big business the way most people think of it, but from everything I heard it was a decent livelihood for most of the vendors.

I was halfway into a dream that made me smile when Pauli punched me again. He was really beginning to piss me off, and the bruise on my left arm grew with each punch.

"Now what?"

"One of Escobar's trucks just came into a back bay."

I looked through one of the big doors and decided Pauli must have X-ray vision to see through all the crap inside the building.

"The tan one with the eagle on the side. See it?" he asked as I picked up the camera and used the lens as binoculars.

Peering through the eyepiece of the camera, I panned the camera around until I found the truck he had described. "Got it," I said. "Now what?"

"Keep watching it. If anything but lettuce comes out the rear, take its picture."

A 500-millimeter lens isn't designed to be hand-held. I looked around the car and found an old oil rag on the back floorboard. Folding it to make a pad, I laid it on the dashboard and rested the camera lens on it.

"Pretty chancy bringing illegals through in broad daylight," I said as I watched.

"Best time. So many fuckin' Mexicans around, who's gonna notice five or ten more? Once they're out of the truck, they just blend in. They'd be too easy to spot if they brought them in before the Terminal opened. Might as well carry a sign sayin' 'arrest me.'"

The truck backed into a vacant space and stopped. Two men climbed out of the cab and went to the rear of the truck. It looked like another lettuce day to me. The driver and his passenger were talking and laughing as they pushed the backdoor of the truck open.

"Well, there's a face I recognize," I said as I snapped three or four pictures.

"Who is it?"

"One of them is that guy who was with Escobar at Consuela's."

"Ernesto Lopez. Saw his sheet yesterday while you were in Austin. He's an Escobar-in-trainin'. Petty criminal until recently."

"In the gang?"

"Absolutely. But not into the street stuff anymore. That's for the new punks. Ernesto's workin' on his management skills now. Anything in the truck?"

"Don't see anything."

"Watch under the truck."

I took my eye away from the camera and looked at him.

"For what? An oil leak?"

"Just watch," he said with a smile.

Ernesto and his companion began unloading cases of lettuce and Ruby Red grapefruit. I hadn't eaten since the night before and looking at the produce was making me hungry. As I continued watching, I couldn't believe my eyes.

"What the hell..."

"Trapdoor in the floor of the truck, right? A friend over at INS told me about them. See if you can get pictures of whatever pops up."

Eight shots later I didn't see any more leaks under the

truck. Eight men had slid out from under the truck and rolled out onto the floor of the Terminal within a minute and walked away.

"Remember those faces," Pauli instructed as he started the car and pulled quickly away from the curb.

We went around the block, looking into bay doors as we went. I spotted three of the men leaving the Terminal and walking down the alleyway behind it. They weren't carrying anything with them, and Pauli told me their bags were probably still in the truck. The men entered the backdoor of a building a block from the Terminal as Pauli wrote down the address and returned to our original parking place.

Two hours later, Lopez and his companion were joined by another trio of men. Lopez and his buddy climbed back into the truck and pulled away from the stall, leaving the other three with the produce boxes.

"Showtime," Pauli said as he shifted the car into gear.

He kept us a block and a half behind Lopez's truck. Lopez pulled over at the front entrance of the building we had seen the illegals enter and honked once. A few seconds later, all eight men came out of the building and climbed back into the truck, as I continued capturing them on film. We followed the truck through the San Antonio streets until we hit an on-ramp for the interstate.

"Might as well settle back and relax," Pauli said as he readjusted himself behind the wheel. "Just hope we don't wind up in Bumfuck, Iowa."

An hour later, we were approaching Mountain View. We pulled over and waited as the truck stopped at the main gate of ABP. I rested the camera on the dashboard again and continued my chronicle of events. The gates closed behind the van as it entered the main parking area. Stopping near the front door of the company, Lopez jumped out of the truck cab and bounded up the front steps. Ten minutes later, he came out of the building accompanied by Camarena, and I got a nice shot of them together.

"I'd like to get Camarena's attention," I said. "Let him know that I know what his game is."

"What good would that do?"

"We need to flush him out, get him to make a move."

"The only move you might get is a bunch of guys reachin' in their pockets for pistolas."

"Well, we're not getting anywhere with this undercover shit."

Pauli started the car again and made a U-turn to drive away from the plant. "Don't worry, Jo. You'll have everything you need in a day or so. I guarantee it."

He didn't offer any more details, but I knew there was something Pauli hadn't told me. He drove back to San Antonio with a shit-eatin' grin on his face. He didn't stop again until he pulled into a fast food place not far from his house and picked up a bucket of chicken. We still had some telephone work to do.

Pauli made a couple of calls, putting out a search for information about Pan American Investments and then turned the phone over to me. I wasn't looking forward to making my call.

"Hello," a man's voice answered.

"Mr. McCaffrey?" I asked, almost hoping it wasn't.

"Yes, this is Albert McCaffrey. Who is this?"

"My name is Joanna Carlisle, sir, and I'm a reporter. I was wondering if I could ask you a few questions about your daughter, Julianne."

There was silence on the other end of the line for several uncomfortable moments.

"You say you're a reporter?" he finally asked.

"Yes, sir. I'm researching a story, and during my investigation, I came across the story of your daughter's death."

"It's been a long time, Ms. Carlisle."

"I know, and I apologize for dragging up unpleasant memories. Is there anything you can tell me about your daughter's death that might not have been in the police reports?"

"I doubt it. They never found out who killed her, but I believe they were very thorough. Just ran into a brick wall."

"The newspaper report said she had been at a fraternity party. Do you know whether that's true or not?"

"I assume it is. She was engaged to a member of the fraternity. Her fiancé told me they had gone to the party but left early. He was coming down with a touch of the flu or something, so he took her back to her apartment and went on home."

"Well, that sounds pretty much like what the police told me. I was hoping there might have been something they left out. I appreciate you talking to me about this, Mr. McCaffrey."

"You know, I've always hoped they would find whoever killed my daughter. If something should come up, I hope you'll let me know."

"I will, sir. And thank you again."

It was nearly ten o'clock before Pauli and I finished eating and putting together what we had. We knew that Lopez was one of Escobar's men and that Escobar and Camarena were related. Now we knew that Lopez had delivered illegals directly into Camarena's hands at ABP. What we didn't have was proof that Camarena knew they were illegals. We assumed they had picked up forged papers in San Antonio and that would let Camarena plead ignorance. I felt like a dog chasing its tail and was ready to pack it in for the night. We put the McCaffrey case into another folder and decided it was a separate story that might merit closer examination at another time.

Pauli and I were finishing one last cup of coffee when we heard a banging at the front door.

"You expectin' someone?" Pauli asked as he glanced at his wristwatch.

I shook my head. "No one knows I'm here except Cate."

"I'm not expecting anyone until tomorrow," he said as he rose from his chair. He stopped on his way to the door to take a handgun from a hall desk. Looking through the peephole in the door, he turned around and motioned to me. "It's for you."

While he returned the gun to the desk, I opened the front door and saw Kyle standing on Pauli's front steps.

"You looking for me?" I asked.

"Mom told me where you were."

"What can I do for you?"

"I want you to get the fuck out of my life! I didn't need you then, and I don't need you now. All you've done is cause more trouble!" he rambled irrationally.

Looking past him, I saw Sarita leaning against the car. Tearstains ran down her olive face, leaving traces of salt in their path. Pushing past Kyle, I went to Sarita's side and helped her into the house. Her body trembled as I put my arm around her and guided her toward the couch. Pauli appeared from nowhere carrying a First Aid kit and wet washcloth. There was a small cut under her right eye, and the blood from it had mingled with her tears. Pauli spoke to her in a soft voice as he wiped her face. I knew she was in better hands than mine and turned to face Kyle, who had slumped down on the couch. Deciding the best thing I could do was find out what had happened, I led him into the kitchen and set a cup of coffee in front of him.

"What happened?" I asked.

"Four men. They grabbed Sarita outside our apartment building and used her to get inside."

"A robbery?"

"A warning," he said, his eyes hard as he looked at me. "To drop the story. I didn't understand half of what they were saying, but I got the message. You're still investigating, aren't you?"

"Yes, but..."

"Well, tonight Sarita paid for your damn digging, okay?"

"I haven't been near either one of you."

"The message is 'lay off or next time it won't just be a warning.' I told them I didn't know anything. That's when they told me to pass the message on to you. Then they made sure I understood."

"What did they do to Sarita?"

"Two of them held me while the other two hit her," he said without looking at me, his voice shaking. "Then they tore her clothes off, and there wasn't a goddamn thing I could do to help her."

"Did they..."

"No, but they could have. One of them said, 'next time.'" He tried to control himself, but his emotions were getting the best of him. He threw his coffee cup across the kitchen, and it shattered against the wall.

"We have to get you and Sarita out of San Antonio," I said.

I left the kitchen and went into Pauli's office. In less than twenty minutes, I had reservations for both of them on the last flight to Dallas that night and had spoken to Sarita's mother, who agreed to pick them up when the plane landed. In Kyle's condition, I couldn't be sure he hadn't been followed to Pauli's house.

When I returned to the living room, Pauli was covering Sarita with an afghan.

"We don't have time for that, Pauli. We have to be at the

airport in half an hour. Can you make it by then?"

"With time to spare. What's goin' on?"

I took him aside and recounted what Kyle had told me. While I got Sarita up, Pauli grabbed a jacket and took his pistol from the drawer again, checking to see how many rounds he had. We led Kyle and Sarita through the backdoor into the garage and got into Pauli's car. He told them to lie down so they couldn't be seen from the outside before he pushed the button on the garage door opener and backed out. He drove slowly for several blocks, constantly checking to see if we were being followed. When he was satisfied we were alone, he floored the accelerator and headed toward the San Antonio airport, making it with time to spare. Pauli hung back as I escorted them into the terminal.

"I should stay here," Kyle said.

"There's nothing you can do here. Sarita needs you with her." I took him by the arm and pulled him toward me. "Nothing is more important now than Sarita's safety, Kyle. Maybe I should have realized this could happen, but I thought they would come after me directly. I'm sorry. I know I said I wouldn't steal your story, but it's out of our hands now. I have to take it to the end. I hope you can understand that."

He looked at me and nodded.

"I'll let you know when you can come back and write it up."

"I'm not sure I care about it anymore."

I waited until they had passed safely through airport security before I rejoined Pauli.

"I know that look," he said. "You got a plan."

"Yeah."

He stopped and shifted his cigar in his mouth. The truth was that I didn't have a plan, but if vengeance belonged to the Lord, I wanted to be His messenger. I hadn't met Felix Camarena personally. Maybe it was time to do that.

Chapter
Twenty-Two

I COULDN'T SLEEP that night, but this time I didn't notice Pauli's intermittent snoring. I poured over the files we were accumulating, trying to decide what to do next. I had seen or been seen by almost everyone involved in the story. Camarena had possibly seen me at Mountain View before Lena was killed, but I couldn't be sure. Pauli had noted Camarena's San Antonio address in the file. Unfolding a city map of San Antonio, I found the street. It was in a section of the city that I recognized as an older but affluent part of town. Over the years, the homes in the area had matured, and the value of the property had remained expensive and stable.

I left Pauli's house before the sun came up and less than forty minutes later was driving into the neighborhood known as Hacienda Heights. Unlike Austin, where there is a twenty-four-hour-a-day traffic jam, early morning San Antonio traffic took a rest. I couldn't help but reflect that it had been a peaceful city before the nearly one million inhabitants turned it into just another big city. I found Buena Vista without difficulty and drove slowly down the tree- and hedge-lined street until I saw the number 424 illuminated on a brick pillar that supported an ornate, wrought iron security gate. It was nearly dawn on a Saturday morning as I pulled to the curb a block down the street from the Camarena house. Pouring a cup of coffee from the Thermos I borrowed from Pauli, I waited. I didn't know what I expected but wanted to know more about Camarena's routine.

My life had been disrupted more than I thought was possible in the short time since Cate came to me looking for help. I was more exhausted than I realized, and the warm coffee was making me drowsy. Rolling down the window to let fresh air into the car, I wondered whether I would be doing what I was doing now if I had made a different choice fifteen years earlier. I could have had a safe, peaceful life secure in the arms of a woman who loved me, or I could have had a life wandering from place to place seeking danger and excitement. I had chosen the latter. Now I desperately wanted that safe, peaceful, secure life, yet here I was wandering around a city I barely knew with danger seeking me, and it wasn't the least bit exciting. Part of me was angry that Cate had dragged me into this mess, but I knew I would have done the same thing if our roles had been reversed. She had never asked anything of me before, and I could have turned her down. But I didn't. Now I had to force Cate out of my mind and remember Lena and the look on Sarita's face. I had always done my best work when I was pissed off. I had already surpassed that point and moved on to a higher level of anger.

My train of thought was interrupted by a thumping sound at the rear of my Blazer that nearly caused me to spill my coffee. Glancing quickly in the rearview mirror I groaned when I saw blue and red police lights flashing behind me. Great! Just fucking wonderful. A moment later an officer's face appeared in the driver's side window, his hand resting on the grip of his service revolver.

"Can I help you, officer?" I asked.

"License and registration, ma'am."

I reached across the front seat and flipped open the glove compartment, rummaging around a few minutes before I located my vehicle registration. Without thinking I reached toward my back pocket to retrieve my license.

"Freeze!" he said loudly and plainly as I found myself looking into the barrel of his forty-five. "Let me see both hands."

"No problem, officer. My license is in my wallet in my back pocket."

"Put your left hand out the window and open the door with your right. Then step out of the car," he ordered, moving slightly away from the door.

I kept my hands raised as I stepped slowly from the Blazer. "I'm sorry, officer. I wasn't thinking."

"Take your wallet from your pocket using only your

thumb and forefinger."

Nodding, I handed him my wallet, keeping my eyes on his revolver.

"Move to the back of your vehicle and place your hands above the tailgate."

Watching Camarena's house through the windows of my SUV, I waited while the patrolman called my license and plates in to his dispatcher. A few minutes later he said, "You can lower your hands, Ms. Carlisle. Why are you parked in this neighborhood this early?"

I rubbed my hands together as blood began flowing into my arms again. "I'm a photographer and have an assignment to photograph some of the older homes in this area for a magazine layout. I thought catching a few shots as the sun rose over their rooflines would create some interesting pictures."

"Next time make sure you notify the homeowners' association in advance. Some of the residents around here get pretty jumpy when they spot a vehicle that doesn't belong here."

"I should have thought of that, I guess. Must be a very safe place to live."

Touching the bill of his cap with his fingertips the officer smiled and returned to his patrol car. I was reaching for the handle of my vehicle when I heard a grating, metallic sound. The sun was beginning to filter through the trees as I looked around to find the source of the sound. The gate in front of Camarena's house was swinging open.

Goddamn it! Turning back to the patrol car I called out, "Excuse me, officer!"

Stopping with one foot already in his car, the police officer said, "Ma'am?"

"Can you tell me the fastest way from here to Broadway? I have another assignment after I finish here and don't want to be late."

"Go straight down this street for three blocks and take a left. That street will lead to the northbound interstate. Just watch for the Broadway exit. It's about six miles or so."

Glancing over my shoulder, I looked in the direction he had suggested. Camarena's white Lincoln was already making a right turn three blocks ahead. I waved as the patrol car pulled around me to continue on his search for cars that didn't belong in the area. I pulled away from the curb to find the Lincoln. I hadn't seen who was in the vehicle and hoped it wasn't Mrs. Camarena on her way to an early morning mass.

Although traffic began picking up once I left Hacienda Heights, I didn't have any trouble spotting the Lincoln again. Less than three miles from the house, the car swung into a city park and joined a dozen or so other cars in a grassy parking area. I slowed and saw Felix Camarena getting out of his car, followed by a young boy of about nine. From the way the boy was dressed, it appeared there was going to be an early soccer match. I parked and pulled my camera bag from the backseat of my car.

When I reached the soccer field, I saw two or three dozen people standing along the sidelines and sitting on folding chairs. The game was just beginning, and they were already whooping it up, shouting encouragement at two dozen miniature Peles. I spotted Camarena standing along the sideline, clapping and periodically leaning over to say something to another parent. I don't know shit about soccer and frankly never saw the point of the game. It required speed and agility, but I couldn't think of a single profession that required nimble footwork and forbid you to use your hands. Well, maybe a tap dancer, but then I didn't know anyone making a fortune at that either.

I snapped a telephoto lens onto my camera and used it to find the boy I had seen get out of Camarena's car. When I finally found him, he was running down the field with the ball in front of him, trying to avoid other players rushing around him. I hadn't shot sports in years. Most of the people I took pictures of had been fairly stationary, either because they were ducking for cover or were dead. The little guys on the soccer field were far from dead. I panned Camarena's kid as he moved down the field and was intercepted by a bigger boy.

I shot pictures of several of the boys and had to smile when they scored. The looks on their faces were animated, and their excitement was genuine, unlike professional athletes who are expected to score points and have long since lost the joy of winning for the sake of winning. After a short break, the second half of the game got underway. I was rewinding a roll of film and holding a new roll in my mouth when someone tapped me lightly on the shoulder. I glanced back and saw Camarena standing behind me.

"Getting any good shots?" he asked with a smile.

"I won't know until I develop them."

"Are you a parent?"

"No. Just happened to notice the game and stopped. Pretty fast moving and I thought I could use the practice."

"Felix Camarena," he said, extending a well-manicured hand to me. "My son is number four in the blue and yellow. I'd be interested in getting some pictures of him playing. Some of the other parents might also."

"Well, I hadn't planned to sell them. Like I said, I'm just getting a little practice with action shots. They might not be any good, but I'd be glad to send them to you if they turn out."

"Great!" he said with a broad smile. "You know, you could probably pick up quite a bit of money by taking pictures at games like this."

"Think so?"

"Sure! Everyone wants pictures of their kids."

"I suppose that's true. I hadn't thought about it."

"You have kids?"

"A son. But he's grown now. Wish I had more pictures of him when he was younger."

"See what I mean? Once they're grown, all mama and papa have left are pictures."

"Or if something should happen to them before they get grown. I almost lost mine not long ago."

Camarena shuddered and looked out at the field. "I don't know what I would do if anything happened to Marco."

"I'll see if I can get some good shots of your kid," I said as I advanced the film. I reached into my camera bag and pulled out a notepad and a pencil. "Write your name and where you want the pictures sent. Probably be a few days though."

"Listen, send me all the pictures you think are any good, and I'll get them to the other parents."

"Okay."

"I didn't catch your name," he said as he wrote.

"Joanna Carlisle," I said matter-of-factly as I looked through the viewfinder of the Minolta and refocused the lens.

Camarena's hand made an almost imperceptible pause as it wrote, but he didn't look at me. He was smiling as he handed the pad back to me. We were now formally introduced.

I left before the game ended and returned to Pauli's house.

"Where the hell have you been?" he demanded.

"Watching a soccer game. What's for breakfast?"

"Shit, Jo, you done missed breakfast. About time for lunch."

Over a couple of sandwiches, I told him what I had done, and I could tell that he wasn't happy about it,

"Look," I said, "Kyle and Sarita are out of town. There's nobody here now except me."

"Thanks a lot. I'll remember that when they're blastin' the plaster off my house."

"I can move to a motel if that makes you feel safer."

"Then I'd just have to go over and identify your body. It don't matter anyway. We'll have the rest of this nailed down by tonight anyway. I hope."

That was twice he had alluded to an end to the story and hadn't elaborated. But I had learned a long time ago not to push Pauli for information. When he thought you needed to know, he told you. He finished his sandwich and cleaned up the kitchen.

"You look beat, Jo. Why don't you take a nap for an hour or so? We have to meet someone later, and I don't want you dead on your feet."

I was full of coffee but too exhausted for it to be effective. He promised to wake me later. I wasn't sure what time it was when I heard the phone ring, but I felt better. I went to the bathroom and threw water on my face. I hoped Pauli was right, and it would all be over soon.

When I went into the living room, he was hunched over a pad writing down whatever was being said over the phone. He grunted and nodded and wrote. He looked up as I sat down on the couch and rested my feet on the coffee table.

He covered the mouthpiece with a meaty hand and said, "Get your stuff. We're leaving in a few minutes."

By the time I returned, he was shoving his revolver into a holster.

"Where to?" I asked.

"Meetin' a friend."

"You know, Pauli, this secrecy crap is getting old. Do

you have a secret hand signal I should know about, too?"

"Yeah," he said, sticking his middle finger toward me. "Now let's get out of here."

He didn't seem to be worried about being followed as he left the house and headed for our secret rendezvous. While he tried to control the car with one hand, he felt around in the pocket of his jacket and pulled out a piece of paper.

Tossing it at me, he said, "Got the info on Pan American Investments."

"That the phone call?"

"Yeah. I think you'll find it interesting."

Pauli's scribbles were hard to read, but it didn't take me long to see what he meant. "What do you figure it means?" I asked.

"Blackmail comes to mind," he answered.

"For the McCaffrey girl?"

"Probably. The way I see it, Bradley must have had a hand in the girl's death, either accidentally or on purpose. Don't matter. Anyway, Camarena helped cover it up, and Bradley's been paying for his silence ever since."

"But Pan American went out of business a long time ago."

"True. Might have been set up just to cover the college thing. But now Susan is well off enough to pay Camarena herself. That's probably how Camarena got into ABP in the first place. Bradley is their tax attorney, and we know from your ex that they were her clients when she started working with her. Suppose Camarena used Bradley to get in with ABP so he could pull off his illegal scam? He could use his connection with Escobar to bring them in and make out like the freakin' Frito Bandito."

"Do you think Susan knows about the illegals?"

"Probably, at least covering it up on the books. Maybe she's not making cash payments to Camarena anymore, and the covering up part is the payment."

"I can't believe anyone would pay blackmail for, what, twenty-five years."

"How long would you pay to keep from going to prison for life, or worse?"

"But there's barely even circumstantial evidence that Susan Bradley might have been involved in the girl's death."

"Girl   dies.   Then   a   month   later   Pan   American

Investments, a wholly owned subsidiary of Bradley and Associates, creates a privately endowed scholarship for one Felix Camarena. Face it, you said Camarena wasn't exactly an honor student. You don't have to be a fuckin' genius to think that it was a payoff for something more serious than plagiarism."

"I wish there was something more concrete."

"After twenty years, you ain't gonna find a smokin' gun. You'll just have to take what you get and run with it."

"Yeah, but it's a different story. Right now, I want to nail Camarena for the illegals, Lena's death, and the attack on Sarita."

"I can get you the illegals. Can't guarantee the rest unless somebody rolls over on Camarena. He wouldn't have done it himself." He pulled into a police substation and parked.

"This is where the secret meeting is going to take place? The police department."

"I never said it was a secret meeting," he huffed as he hoisted himself out of the Chrysler.

Chapter
Twenty-Three

I FOLLOWED PAULI into the front entrance of the San Antonio Police Department building. He greeted the desk officer and swapped a few one-liners with other officers as we went down a hallway and stopped outside an interrogation room. He knocked on the door, which was opened immediately by a Hispanic man in his mid-thirties, dressed in dirty jeans and a plaid shirt. His hair was shiny black and long enough to touch the collar of his shirt. He grinned when he saw Pauli, and his teeth were toothpaste commercial white under a thick black mustache that hid his upper lip. He hugged Pauli, and after a few seconds of mutual backslapping, we all made it into the room and closed the door behind us.

"I want to thank you for that all-expense-paid trip to Mexico, Pauli. Not exactly how I planned to spend my vacation, but it's been interesting."

"Thought you'd like it," Pauli said. Turning to me, he said, "Jo, meet Artie Reyna."

As we shook hands, Reyna looked at Pauli. "This the one I went undercover for?"

"Yeah. She's a pain in the ass like you, but still a friend."

Reyna laughed, pulled out a chair, and sat down at the table.

"Artie here was the last partner I had before I retired," Pauli said.

"You should see the moron they got me partnered with now," Reyna said as he lit a cigarette. "Thinks he's fuckin' Rambo."

"You had the police working on the story?" I asked.

"Sort of in an unofficial capacity," Pauli said. "Artie was in that truck we followed a couple of days ago."

"He's working at ABP?"

"Yeah, and if I stay there much longer I'll never appreciate the way a woman smells again. Thinkin' about givin' up steak for Lent." Reyna chuckled.

"Tell Jo what you know," Pauli said.

"I went down to Mexico and contacted a few people in a village there about gettin' into the States. They put me onto this guy, Lopez, and said he'd been in the village lookin' for workers. So I waited and sure enough, he showed up, spreadin' the word about good jobs in El Norte. I paid him three to get me across the border and to San Antonio. There were seven others, and the price was the same for each of them."

"What about once you reached here?" I asked.

"After I finished pickin' lettuce outta my teeth, we went to that building behind the Produce Terminal where we shelled out another five to a guy named Escobar for papers. Social Security, driver's license, the usual stuff. Looked good enough to fool even me. Then this Lopez picked us up again, and we went to ABP. He's a real freak, Pauli. I overheard him talkin' to another guy in the truck about wishin' there had been a couple of women in our group. So they could stop and get a little, you know? Pretty neat little deal. I mean, ain't like no illegal is goin' to the cops to report a rape or anything."

"Did you meet Camarena?" I asked.

"Yeah, at the plant, but just for a few minutes. He checked our teeth and papers, asked a couple of dumbass questions and trotted us off to work. Jesus, even cops don't work hours like that. And good pay, now there's a joke. Hell, I couldn't make the payments on my Camaro with what they were payin'."

"What else did you find out?" Pauli asked.

"I talked to as many people as I could in two days, Pauli. Close as I can figure out from what the other workers told me, Lopez is a real busy boy. Makes a trip to the border a couple of times a week, and his ain't the only truck. Over a few beers they told me some of the trucks are bigger and go farther north."

"From your truck alone, they took in around sixty-five hundred. Do they always bring in eight?" I asked.

"Stick in more'n that and there wouldn't be room to breathe. I was pretty squashed as it was."

I doodled around with a few figures on a piece of paper.

"That's over half a million a year just from one truck," I said.

"Okay, Artie, go home and take a hot shower," Pauli said. "You stink."

"Shit! You mean my vacation is over?" Reyna said.

"Looks like. You think any of the workers at ABP would testify if someone pressed charges against Lopez or Camarena?"

"I doubt it, but there might be some in Mexico who would. Lots of guys runnin' around down there without all their fingers because of the work they did. Once they got hurt, the company didn't keep them on, and some of them are a little pissed about it."

"I'll call you later if we need their names," Pauli said, getting up. "Enjoy the rest of your vacation." When Pauli and I were alone, he asked, "Got enough now?"

"Pretty close. There still isn't any proof that Camarena knew your friend there might have been an illegal. He looked at fake papers, which he could have believed were the real thing."

"Yeah, I guess it is kinda normal to hire workers outta the back of a lettuce truck. Come on, Jo! You got it all on film. Camarena was waitin' for them."

"I know it, and you know it, but will a jury see it?"

"Well, I think they might be a tad suspicious."

"You tell me, Pauli. If you took what we've got right now to the DA, would he go to the grand jury?"

"Probably not."

"Maybe it's just Lopez and Escobar who're involved."

"Look at Lena's notes, Jo. Camarena's name is all over them. If Artie stayed longer at ABP, I'm sure he would've found something on Camarena, too."

"No, he's done enough. Why didn't you tell me you sent someone in there?"

"Because if someone had snagged you and beat the shit out of you like they did your housekeeper, I didn't want Artie compromised. You couldn't tell what you didn't know."

"Won't they miss Reyna now?"

"There's a thousand more out there ready to take his

place. Besides, it ain't like they'd expect him to give two weeks notice."

"Where'd he get the eight hundred?"

"I gave it to him. But don't worry, I won't charge you any interest."

IT WAS ALREADY dark by the time we picked up dinner and pulled into Pauli's driveway. As his headlights swept over the front of the house, I thought I saw someone in the shadows next to his front door. I turned to look at Pauli and before I could say anything, he said, "I saw him."

The garage door opened, and we pulled in. Pauli threw the car into park, pulling his gun as he exited the car. The garage door was halfway down when he ducked under it. I jumped out of the car and went through the kitchen toward the front door. As I opened the door, I saw Pauli holding a man against the side of the house, his gun under the man's chin.

"Flip on the light, Jo!" Pauli yelled.

As soon as the light came on, Pauli loosened his grip on the man and reholstered his pistol.

"That's a good way to get yourself killed, kid," he said as he turned to come up the steps of the house."

I looked over the edge of the porch and saw Kyle leaning against the brick wall.

"What the hell are you doing here? You're supposed to be with Sarita."

He pushed away from the wall and came to the foot of the steps. "Can I come in?" he asked, rubbing his chin where Pauli had had his gun pressed.

I didn't answer him but went back into the house, leaving the front door partially open. Goddamn kids never do what the hell you tell them. I joined Pauli in the kitchen as he spread food on the table. Kyle stood in the doorway and watched us for a few minutes.

"Sit down, kid," I finally said. "I'll split my burger with you."

He sat down and took the food I handed him.

"How'd you get back?" I asked.

"Flew in and took a cab from the airport."

"I hope you had the brains to leave Sarita with her folks."

"She's going to stay there until this is over. We both thought I should come back."

"You're both wrong," I said, shaking my head.

"It's my story. If I don't put it to bed, Sarita and I will never feel safe again. I don't want her spending all her time looking over her shoulder."

"Might be doin' that anyway," Pauli interjected. "You put Escobar and Lopez away, the rest of their friends might still come lookin' for you."

"We're leaving San Antonio as soon as the story breaks. We've been planning it for a while, but this kind of cinched it for us."

"Giving up journalism?" I asked.

He shook his head as he chewed. "Been offered a job with the Denver Post."

"Nice state," I said with a smile. "Took your mother up there once. She didn't enjoy it nearly as much as I did."

"Was that when the groundhog got her?" Kyle asked as he chewed his burger.

"She told you about that?" I asked, more than a little surprised.

"I overheard her telling the story to someone else."

"What's the groundhog story?" Pauli said through a mouthful of food.

"Oh, I dragged Cate on a camping expedition to Colorado. You know, a little fishing, a little relaxation, a little tent. She only went along because I wanted to go. It was colder than a well digger's ass at night, and the last night we were there it was colder than usual. Anyway, one thing led to another in the sleeping bag when, right in the middle of all that passion, we were rudely interrupted at an inopportune moment by a damn groundhog looking for fresh air. Poked Cate right in the back. She screamed, and needless to say, we kinda lost the moment. Never got her to go camping again."

Pauli started laughing and I smiled at the memory. When I looked at Kyle, he was smiling, too.

"You want me to catch you up on what we've got so far?" I asked Kyle. "We've come to an impasse. Maybe you can come up with a fresh idea."

We sat down on Pauli's couch, and I took him through everything we had gathered, one piece of paper at a time, even the possible connection between Susan, Camarena, and

McCaffrey. He didn't say much as I explained what we thought was going on, only nodding occasionally. When we were finished, he rested his elbows on his knees and looked at me.

"I didn't see much evidence that would involve Camarena with the illegals," he said.

"It's our weakest point, but I don't know what else we can do."

"You sure can't ask Susan. If she was involved in the McCaffrey thing, she'd cover for Camarena to save her own ass anyway. If we could sneak a peek at her files on ABP, we might be able to find out whether the company was actually paying to have the illegals brought in."

I opened another file folder and handed it to him. He glanced over the pages quickly.

"How'd you get these?" he asked.

"Don't ask."

"What about these 'Miscellaneous Expenditures'? Any idea what they are?"

"Nope. I gave them to an accountant friend of mine in Kerrville, but he told me what I already knew. Could be anything."

"So if the company was paying someone to bring illegals in, it could be covered under miscellaneous."

"That would be my guess. Unfortunately, it would take a court order to dredge up all the files on ABP."

"Maybe it's one of those implied things. You know, like Reagan and the Contras. Not a direct order, just a heavy-duty suggestion."

"The company says it wishes it had more workers and is willing to pay a bonus to anyone who can provide them," I pondered aloud.

"Then Camarena sees the chance to make some bucks from both ends of the pipeline. The company pays him for finding workers, and the workers pay him for finding them jobs. All he had to do was find someone to actually bring them in," Kyle continued.

"So he turns to his cousin, Escobar, and they set up the pipeline."

"Makes sense to me, but the paper trail would be a bitch to follow."

"I got a load of illegals on film a couple of days ago. I haven't developed the film yet, but it covers the line from

San Antonio to Mountain View."

"Can you develop them here?"

I shook my head. "I've got a darkroom at the ranch, but nothing here."

"Then let's go to the ranch."

"Not safe. After I showed my hand with Camarena, someone might be watching the house."

"What about the darkroom at the Light? The building's open all night."

Two hours later, Kyle and Pauli waited while I processed the pictures. After placing the prints in the dryer, I joined them in the newsroom.

"You got 'em?" Pauli asked.

"They're in the dryer. Be about another ten minutes."

Kyle went into the darkroom, and I sat down in a chair next to Pauli.

"What're you gonna do with all this shit now?" he asked.

"Let Kyle write his story and turn everything over to INS, the DA, and whoever the hell else wants it, I guess."

"The DA won't want the story released until he has time to round up a few people."

"It'll take a day or so to write it up properly. Once it's edited and fact-checked, they can break the story any time. By then there shouldn't be any reason to target anyone. The whole world will know what's going on."

Kyle came out of the darkroom carrying a stack of pictures.

"That all of them?" I asked.

"Yeah. Who's this guy?"

I took the picture, and he pointed out Lopez standing behind his truck at the Produce Terminal. Pauli leaned over to look and recognized Lopez before I did.

"Ernesto Lopez," Pauli said. "One of Escobar's flunkies."

"He was one of the men who attacked Sarita," Kyle said flatly.

"You sure?" I asked.

"I'm not likely to forget any of them. They didn't try to hide their faces. But this guy Lopez, he really enjoyed what he was doing."

"Did he seem to be in charge, or did he take orders from one of the others?" Pauli asked.

"He wasn't in charge. One of the men was older. He seemed to be in control, but he had a hard time with this one."

"Can you describe the older man?" Pauli continued.

"Maybe mid to late forties, graying black hair, mustache," Kyle said.

"Could be half the spics in San Antonio," Pauli said.

"Guess I'm not as sure about the other three, but I really watched this Lopez. He didn't want to stop when the older guy told him to. He was ready to rape her."

"Sounds like what Reyna said about him," I said to Pauli.

Kyle closed his eyes and kept talking. "They argued about it in Spanish. Sarita was crying. The other two were holding her down on the floor, and Lopez kept looking at her and arguing with the older man. He called him something. Sounded like Ricky or Rico. Something like that."

"Frederico Escobar," Pauli said with a smile.

"But you called him Freddie," I said.

"Just because he hates being called Freddie," Pauli answered. He looked at Kyle. "If you saw a picture of this older man, think you could ID him?"

"Absolutely."

Pauli stopped at the police department long enough to appropriate a picture of Escobar. Without the slightest hesitation, Kyle picked him from a group of ten mug shots that Pauli handed him. We might never get Camarena, but we had Lopez and Escobar by the balls. We celebrated over enchiladas and Coronas before driving to Pauli's again.

Chapter
Twenty-Four

PAULI OFFERED KYLE the use of his computer to write the story then contacted Reyna to give him the good news about Lopez. We had a witness to the attack on Sarita, and a witness to the smuggling of illegals and the sale of fake government documents. Kyle could return to Sarita, and they could plan to live happily ever after in Colorado. The story would help assure his future, and as I watched him putting it together, I felt something I had never felt before — pride. He had stuck it out until the end, even though I knew from long experience that every instinct was telling him to run.

Pauli was at the sink chopping lettuce and whistling softly to himself when I went into the kitchen for another cup of coffee.

"How's it going?" he asked as I poured.

"It's going to be a great story. Wish we could have tied up everything, but this will be good enough."

"If the Feds take a serious interest in Camarena, maybe they can nail his ass, too."

I shrugged and sipped at the coffee. The phone rang, and Pauli wiped his hands on a dishtowel before answering it. He listened for a second and pointed the phone at me.

"It's for you, Jo. Your ex."

I would be glad to finally be able to tell her that everything was fine. That our son was going to be around a while longer. I decided not to tell her about Sarita. It was over, and Sarita hadn't been badly hurt physically. I didn't see any sense in upsetting her over something that couldn't be changed.

"Hi," I said lightly as I took the receiver. "I was going to call you..."

"Jo," she interrupted me. I noticed that her voice sounded different, subdued, like someone trying to find a good way to tell you bad news.

"What's wrong, Cate? Are you all right?"

Pauli swiveled his head around to look at me. I just shrugged. She hadn't said anything yet, but my stomach told me there was a problem.

"Cate? Answer me, honey. What's wrong?"

Her voice was shaking when she finally spoke again. "Susan and I have been abducted, Jo. I'm supposed to read something to you."

"What? By whom?"

"Please, just listen. Put everything you have about the ABP story in a briefcase, and bring it to fifteen-twelve Alameda..."

"Wait, I don't have anything to write on." I looked around and found a pencil and a napkin on the kitchen table.

"Okay." I repeated the address.

"Be there at three o'clock. If you are, Susan and I won't be hurt. And come alone."

"That's only an hour, Cate. Is someone there with you?"

"Yes."

"Hand the phone to whoever it is."

I heard a man's accented voice as she apparently tried to give him the phone and then what sounded like a slap.

"Cate! Someone speak to me, goddamn it!"

A man's voice came on the line. "You have one hour, Ms. Carlisle. Do you understand what you're to do?"

"Yeah, but how about we meet someplace a little more neutral?" I stalled.

"Fifty-nine minutes," he said as he hung up.

I slammed the receiver down. When I looked up, Kyle was standing in the doorway to the kitchen. "They have your mother," I said. "And Susan."

"How..."

"Someone had to have seen us together either at the ranch or in Austin. Whether they took her from work or home I'm sure Susan must have been with her. These guys have eyes every goddamn place!"

"What do they want?" Pauli asked.

"Everything we have on the ABP story by three o'clock.

I'm supposed to take it to an address on Alameda." I slid the napkin toward him.

"Fuck, Jo, that's in the middle of Escobar's territory. No one will come out of there alive. It'll take us thirty minutes to get there ourselves."

"Guess they figured we wouldn't have time to call in the cavalry with a deadline like that. Kyle, grab everything and put it in a briefcase or something that looks like a briefcase."

"I'll get the car started," Pauli said.

"I'm supposed to be alone, Pauli."

"Hell, you can't get there in less than an hour alone. I know a few back streets that might save us some time. Hang on a minute." Pauli picked up the phone and dialed. A minute later he was talking to Reyna and relaying what was happening. He hung up without saying goodbye and once again removed his gun from the desk drawer. "I didn't use this damn thing this much when I was active duty," he said as he shoved it into his jacket pocket.

"What about me?" Kyle asked. "I know how to use a gun."

"You're staying here," I said.

"The fuck I am!"

"They just want me, Kyle. As far as they know, you're not even in town."

"I have to be there, and I won't get in the way. I love her, too, Jo."

We really didn't have time to argue. Time was slipping away. Pauli had left the room and returned with what looked like the world's oldest briefcase. He tossed it to Kyle. "Put everything in that," he instructed.

He turned to me and handed me the smallest handgun I'd ever seen. It looked like a toy except it wasn't orange.

"You know they'll search me," I said. "I wouldn't get ten feet with that Tinker Toy."

"There's a slit in the bottom of the briefcase. Slip it in there under the paperwork. Most of these idiots are too lazy to search a bag carefully enough to find it."

"What if I get a real overachiever in the search department?"

"What are you worried about? Either way they're probably gonna kill you, and either way they get the information."

I wasn't feeling any better after a pep talk like that, but we were on our way with fifty minutes left. Pauli planned to stop at the edge of Escobar's territory and let me drive the rest of the way. He and Kyle would have to go the last ten or twelve blocks on foot. I felt certain Kyle could get there but wasn't sure Pauli could walk that far fast enough to make a difference. His size alone would make it hard for him to sneak up on anyone, and I didn't remember seeing a lot of Dempsey Dumpsters the last time we had been in the area.

Pauli pulled over to the curb and shifted his car into park. He turned to me, and his face didn't inspire confidence. "Drive slow. The kid and I have to have enough time to get near the building. If it's the one I think it is, it's sort of a warehouse with lots of open space inside. Stall as much as you can. I don't know how long it will take Reyna to get here."

"Don't come busting in there, Pauli. I can't take the chance Cate will be hurt."

"She'll be okay, Jo. Just stay close to her if you can. She's not the primary target. You are."

Pauli and Kyle got out of the car, with Pauli leading the way. I glanced at my watch, and when they had disappeared around the corner of a building, I pulled away from the curb. Driving slowly, I tried to find numbers on the buildings. I was beginning to get frustrated when I saw a man step out of an alleyway. As I slowed down even further, he moved toward the car. I recognized Lopez as soon as he bent down to look into the car.

"Pull in there," he instructed, pointing to the alleyway.

I went down the alley and stopped about halfway down. As I got out of the car, I looked around at the tops of the buildings lining the alley. I didn't see anything, but that didn't mean there wasn't someone there. Suddenly, Lopez slammed me against the side of the car with enough force to knock the wind out of me. As I gasped for breath, he searched my clothing a little more vigorously than necessary.

"Where's the briefcase?" he asked.

"In the car," I managed to say.

"Get it and let's go."

I reached into the front floorboard and grabbed the briefcase. A few yards down the alley, we turned into a walkway that opened into a small courtyard. Six or seven men stood around and almost came to attention as Lopez and I joined them. Lopez went into a door off the courtyard, and I followed him but was stopped by one of the men before I could enter the door. A moment later, Escobar, trailed by Lopez, came out the door.

"Where's Cate Hammond?" I demanded.

"You search her?" Escobar asked Lopez, who nodded that he had.

"The bag, too?"

"No, not the bag, Rico."

"Then do it now."

I held the bag out and Lopez took it. He opened the bag and dug through the papers inside before closing it and handing it back to me.

"You come alone?" Escobar asked me.

"I did what I was told to do."

Escobar stepped aside and motioned me inside the building. I waited to see if he was going to follow me, but he remained outside with the others. The door opened into a narrow hallway. I didn't see any other doorways leading off the hallway and walked in the only direction left, straight ahead. The hallway was about sixty feet long and led to what appeared to be a cavernous room at the other end.

When I reached the end of the hall, I looked around and saw Camarena standing in front of a table to the left of the doorway. He motioned me forward, and I saw that he was holding a revolver. To my right, Cate and Susan were sitting in chairs, bound and gagged. I started to go to them, but Camarena stopped me.

"They're still breathing. Bring the case to me."

I tried to give Cate a reassuring smile as I turned toward Camarena. As I got closer, he leveled his revolver at me. Reaching the table, I set the briefcase down and stood there looking at him.

"Can we go now?" I asked.

"You can all go in a moment. But first I have to see what you brought."

"So look. It's right there in front of you, asshole."

His jaws tightened, and his knuckles whitened as he gripped the revolver tighter. "You open it," he said.

I opened the briefcase and looked inside, wishing I knew what the hell to do next. "By the way, the pictures of your kid came out better than I thought they would," I said.

"But it kinda looks like you won't be getting them now."

"That's a shame, but I'll survive without them."

"Hope I can say the same," I said, looking at him. I pulled out two manila folders and laid them on the table.

"This it?"

"I put everything on CDs, too," I said, reaching back into the briefcase. I managed to find the slit Pauli had made in the bottom and slid the gun out. I picked up two CDs with the same hand. As I brought my hand out of the briefcase, I dropped the disks on the table, holding only the gun.

He laughed when he saw how small the pistol was. "And what do you think you're going to do with that?"

"I'll blow a hole in your head big enough to look through," I answered, raising the pistol. "All I want is to take Cate and her partner and get out of here unmolested. Now put your gun down on the table, slowly, and back away. You can have this other shit."

He smiled at me in a way that was unnerving, but put the gun down anyway. "And how are you planning to get past the men outside?"

"Well, I haven't quite gotten that far yet, Felix. How about if you come around here so you can escort us out?"

I heard a sound behind me, like a chair moving. I turned halfway to see if Cate was all right but wasn't ready for what I saw. Susan was standing up with a gun in her hand. I glanced at the smiling Camarena and opened my mouth to speak. I never got a word out before Susan fired twice. The first bullet tore into the skin of my right side, and even though it was off the mark, the second shot was good enough to shatter the humerus of my left arm. As I fell, I saw the terrified look on Cate's face as she witnessed what Susan had done.

I fell forward and hit the floor hard but wasn't sure whether I was injured as badly as it felt. I was bleeding profusely and could feel the warmth of my blood as it spread up and down my clothes. It only took a few seconds for my body to react once it recovered from the initial shock of being shot. I closed my eyes against the burning pain in my side and down my arm, deciding that no matter what, playing possum was the only option I had left. I heard footsteps coming toward me. A hand grabbed my shoulder and rolled me halfway over while I held my breath as long as I could.

"You got her, Bradley."

"Can't tell if she's dead or not with all this blood, but she will be soon enough if she keeps bleeding like this."

I was still holding the pistol and allowed Susan to take it from my hand. I could hear my heart beating, rushing blood past my eardrums, and prayed that Pauli would bust through the door in time to save Cate. When the door opened a moment later, I thought my prayers had been answered.

"Everything okay in here?" an accented voice asked.

"Go back outside, Ernesto," Camarena ordered. "Bring my car around. We're almost through. Don't be surprised if you hear a couple more gunshots."

I watched through barely half-opened eyes as Susan began pacing between my body and where Camarena stood. Loss of blood had begun making me dizzy, creating ripples of nausea in my stomach.

"That's a nice souvenir," Camarena said. "Derringer, isn't it?"

"I guess so."

"Good thing we slipped that revolver to you."

"Well, if it weren't for you and that idiot cousin of yours, we wouldn't be in this mess. All you had to do was get rid of Kyle and that would have been the end of it. But no, you had to get cute and send some kindergartner to do it."

"Rico said it was the best way."

"Rico was wrong, Felix!" Susan seethed. "The junior hitman fucked up and brought her into it."

"But we got all the evidence and we'll find the kid. You worry too much."

"One of us has to worry. When there's that much money at stake, you can't be screwing around playing Pancho Villa."

"Don't talk to me like that, Bradley, or..."

"Or what, Felix, you'll tell the police about Julianne?"

"No statute on murder, my friend."

"Well, there is a statute on blackmail, and I'm pretty fucking tired of paying for a dumb mistake."

A moment later I heard two gunshots, followed by the dull thud of a body falling to the ground. Blinking to clear my blurring vision, I saw Camarena's dead eyes looking at me and watched as blood from his body quickly pooled and moved across the floor to mingle with mine. The thought of it made me feel even sicker. Footsteps were moving away from me, and I managed to turn my head to follow them. Susan still carried the revolver as she approached Cate. She knelt down next to her and removed the gag from her mouth. Cate gulped for breath through her mouth as tears ran down her face. Susan reached up to wipe them away, but Cate turned away from her.

"I'm sorry, Cate. I never intended for it to end this way," she said.

Cate's head jerked back toward her. "Why, Susan? I don't understand. You have everything. What could you possibly hope to gain from all this?"

"Felix has been blackmailing me for years. While I was in law school, I got drunk and a girl died, accidentally. He knew and helped cover it up in exchange for money. He was scum, but what choice did I have?"

"You could have gone to the police. If it was an accident..."

"And throw away everything I had worked for? No, thanks."

"You were covering up what he was doing at ABP, too, weren't you?"

"He forced me to, Cate. I wish you could understand."

"I understand you tried to have my son murdered. If he had exposed Camarena, you might have been able to get out from under. You're a respected attorney, Susan. No one would have believed him."

"You're right, but I needed Camarena as a middleman with Escobar." She laughed and stood up. "You can't believe that he was the brains behind the illegal smuggling," she said as she pointed at Camarena's body. "Shit, I practically had to tell him how to set it up. It's worth millions every year and is virtually risk free if it's handled right. But then Kyle had to start poking around. I couldn't take the chance he would stumble onto something. Camarena and Escobar would have turned on me in a heartbeat to save their own asses. Now I only have to worry about Escobar since your dear, departed ex killed Camarena for me."

"You'll be caught eventually. You know that."

"Yeah, but by the time the police sort all this out, I'll be relaxing on a Caribbean beach somewhere. Now you're the only witness. This part I hadn't planned, but good old Jo there didn't leave me any other way out except through you. You're good, Cate, but not good enough to give up millions for."

"And who will get blamed for my murder, Susan?"

"Does it really matter now?" Susan asked as she raised the revolver toward Cate.

Mustering all the strength I could, I hoarsely called her name. She spun around and saw me looking at her.

"Well, you're tougher than you look, Jo," she said as she moved a couple of steps toward me and took aim.

A loud noise assaulted my ears, and I thought she had fired and missed. The noise was followed by the sound of voices yelling. I couldn't keep my eyes open any longer. The last thing I heard was Cate calling my name.

Chapter
Twenty-Five

MY EYES FLEW open, and I felt drenched in sweat. I looked around, trying to help my brain figure out where I was. Then I smelled the scent I hated most in the world and knew instantly. Another fuckin' hospital. My hearing caught up with my sight, and I heard a beeping sound. As I scanned the room, the rate of the beeps increased. I took a deep breath and listened as they slowed. A few seconds later I was blinded by a light and clamped my eyelids closed. Fingers began poking at me, and I heard a strange voice.

"She's awake," a woman said.

"Turn off the goddamn light," I croaked.

The light went off, and I felt warm fingers enclose my right hand. I would have known that touch anywhere and was glad I was still alive to feel it. Warm, sweet breath flowed over my ear.

"Welcome back, Jo," Cate said. "Where have you been?"

"Dreamin' about you and groundhogs, baby," I said.

Her laugh was better medicine than whatever they were pumping into my right arm. I would have given anything to wrap my arms around her and hold her but even small movements made me wince as the tape securing a bandage on my right side pulled against still-tender skin. A dull, throbbing pain assured me that the cast I saw engulfing my left arm and hand wasn't going to allow much mobility for a while either.

"They got anything to drink in this joint?"

She held a straw to my mouth, and I have never tasted better water in my life. The nurse left the room, and we were alone for about ten seconds. Cate left my side and opened the blinds partway to let a little light into the room. Just then the hospital door flew open, and the bulk of Wendell Pauli filled the opening. He came to the side of the bed and patted me hard enough to make me clench my teeth against the pain. "You scared the shit out of us, Carlisle," he said.

"I see you survived," I said.

"Sorry we were a little late gettin' in there. You've missed a bunch since then."

I looked at Cate. "How long?"

"Five days."

"And thanks to that new metal rod holdin' your arm together you can look forward to bein' stopped at every airport security checkpoint in America. You've got a lot of catchin' up to do, girl. You uncovered the ass-kickin' story of the year," Pauli said with a smile.

"Kyle's story."

"Yeah, whatever. Anyway, there are so many people duckin' for cover, you'd think it was huntin' season."

"Just give me the Reader's Digest version."

Cate took my hand again, and I barely heard what Pauli was saying. I hadn't ever seen him so excited. Retirement didn't become either of us.

"We got Lopez and Escobar for attackin' Sarita. We got Lopez for bringin' illegals in and Escobar for sellin' phony documents. Escobar rolled on Camarena's part in the deal, but Camarena already received his sentence. Man, I haven't seen this much finger-pointin' since the last time I went to the symphony. Escobar's talkin' so fast they had to hire an extra stenographer to get it all. He's pointin' all ten fingers at Lopez for Lena's murder, but Lopez ain't goin' down alone. He's takin' Susan Bradley with him on that one. She's gonna wish she'd been killed at the warehouse instead of gettin' a measly flesh wound."

"What?"

"Bradley was in the car with Camarena in Mountain View when you and Lena were talkin' to Juan Doe. Lopez says she ordered you killed, but they got Lena instead. Also chargin' her for conspiracy to kill Kyle. Cate here has turned over all of Bradley's records on ABP to the Feds, and there ain't enough toilet paper in the universe to wipe all the shit off the company managers. They're swearin' on a stack of Good Books that they didn't know nothin' about it, of course. They'll probably get a humongous fine, minimum. Kyle was right about the Reagan-Contra-type thing."

"He's a smart kid," I said. Cate squeezed my hand and smiled.

"Oh, and here's the killer. You ready for this? Susan didn't have a goddamn thing to do with the McCaffrey murder."

"But she said she killed her."

"It was Camarena," Pauli said, shaking his head. "Escobar, during one of his nonstop confession sessions, said Felix told him that he killed the girl. It seems that Susan was drunker than the proverbial skunk that night. When the girl's boyfriend returned her early to her apartment building, Susan made a serious pass at the girl. McCaffrey rejected her and threatened to tell the sorority about Susan's sexual indiscretion. So Bradley smacked her, the girl fell, hit her head, and was out cold. Unfortunately for Bradley, Camarena had finished his shift at the party and was walking home when he saw the argument between Bradley and McCaffrey in front of the building. Being the Good Samaritan and upstanding citizen that he was, he told Susan the girl was dead and offered to dispose of the evidence in exchange for a financial consideration. It turns out the girl wasn't dead until Camarena raped and strangled her."

"Susan paid all those years for something she didn't do," Cate said.

"Correctimundo," Pauli said in triumph.

"I promised to call Mr. McCaffrey," I said.

"Already taken care of. Kyle called," Pauli said with a wave of his hand. He looked at me and smiled. "I got a few things to do, Jo, so I guess I'll let you get back to restin'. Let me know when you're ready, and I'll sneak in some enchiladas and a Corona for you."

"Thanks for everything, Pauli," I said as I shook his hand.

After he left, Cate picked up a newspaper. She helped me hold it up with my good hand as I read the headline "Feds Bust Illegal Smuggling Operation." Beneath the headline the byline read: "Kyle Hammond and Joanna Carlisle."

"It's not my story," I said.

"Don't tell him that. He fought like hell to get your name on the byline since you're not an employee."

Kyle's story recounted the pipeline operation from Mexico to Texas and detailed the involvement of Camarena

and Susan Bradley in Lena's death. In a statement issued by
the federal prosecutor in San Antonio, managers in five
states would be indicted for hiring illegal workers for ABP
production lines and attributed the scheme to a "corporate
greed-driven, national conspiracy." As expected, a
spokesman for American Beef and Pork denied accusations
that the company had conspired to recruit and smuggle
illegal workers into the United States. If such actions had
occurred, however, they were done without the knowledge
of the executives at the Nebraska-based Corporation.

"He was asked to hold to story until today to give
authorities a chance to act," Cate said, giving my free arm a
gentle squeeze. "It was just released today."

I wanted to say how proud I was of our son, but the
muscles in my throat constricted as the unfamiliar emotion
overwhelmed me. Finally managing to clear my throat, I
asked, "Where is he?"

"He spent every night here for the first four days. He
left this morning to pick up Sarita in Dallas. They're flying
back tonight."

"They're moving to Colorado, you know."

"He told me, and it's probably for the best. But don't
worry. I'm sure you two will work out your differences. He
does love you, you know."

"What will you do now, Cate?"

"I haven't decided, but as long as the federal agencies
are going over our files, Bradley and Hammond is closed for
business."

I wished she would take my hand again.

"You're going to be in here a few more days. What are
you going to do after the doctor releases you?"

"Go back to the ranch, I guess. Try to put my life back in
order again."

It wasn't just the tubes in my body that were making me
uncomfortable. She was making me uncomfortable, and I felt
like the rest of my life depended on saying the right thing.
The trouble was I didn't have a clue what the right thing
was.

"You know," I finally said, "it seems like every time
we're together I don't know what to say to you, Cate. But I
don't know why."

"Maybe you won't let your mouth say what your brain
wants it to say."

"Probably," I said with a chuckle that made my side ache beneath my bandage. "I've never had a way with words."

"You used to." She smiled.

She turned to pick up her jacket, but I grabbed her arm to stop her. She turned around, brushing hair away from her face.

"Are you leaving?" I asked.

"I thought I'd go back to my hotel and take a long hot shower and a quick nap. I have to pick up Kyle and Sarita at the airport later."

Using whatever strength I could find, I pulled her closer to me. "Please let me have Sundays again," I begged.

She kissed me softly and, placing her lips close to my ear, whispered, "Sundays have always been yours, Jo."

FORTHCOMING TITLES

published by
Quest Books

IM
by Rick R. Reed

A gay thriller with supernatural overtones, *IM* is the story of a serial killer using a gay hook-up website to prey on young gay men on Chicago's north side. The website's easy and relatively anonymous nature is perfect for a killer.

When the first murder comes to light, the first detective on the scene is Ed Comparetto, one of the police force's only openly gay detectives. He interviews the young man who discovered the body, Timothy Bright, and continues his investigation as the body count begins to rise. But, Comparetto hits a snag when he is abruptly fired from the police force. The cause? Falsifying evidence. It turns out that Timothy Bright has been dead for more than two years, murdered in much the same way as the first victim Ed investigated.

The case becomes a driving force for Comparetto, who finds more and more evidence to support that the person he first spoke to about the murders is really dead. Is he a ghost? Or, is something even more inexplicable and chilling going on? As the murder spree escalates and Comparetto realizes Bright is the culprit, he begins to fear for his own sanity...and his own life. Can Ed race against time and his own doubts to stop the killings before he and his new lover become victims?

Available May 2007

Tears Don't Become Me
by Sharon G. Clark

GW (Georgia Wilhelmina) Diamond, Private Investigator, dealt in missing children cases — only. It didn't alter her own traumatic childhood experience, but she could try to keep other children from the same horrors. She'd left her past and her name behind her. Or so she thought. This case was putting her in contact with people she had managed to keep a distant and barely civil relationship with for fifteen years. Now the buried past was returning to haunt her. When Sheriff Matthews of Elk Grove, Missouri, asked her to take a case involving a teenaged runaway girl, she believed it would be no different from any other. Until Matthews explained she had to take a cop as partner or no deal. A cop who just happened to be the missing girl's aunt.

Erin Dunbar, received the call concerning her niece from an old partner, Frank Matthews. It should have been from her sister, but their estrangement, compounded by her having moved to Detroit, kept that from happening. Now she would have to work with a PI. One had nearly killed her and Frank years ago; she expected this one would be no different. Matters were only made worse by discovering it was a "she" PI — a Looney-tune one who gave new and literal meaning to: "Hands Off." For the sake of her niece, Erin would put up with just about anything, until...GW seemed to be strangely affected by this case and Erin, to her chagrin and amazement, was strangely affected by her.

If Erin could solve GW's past, give her hope, could they have a hope of finding her niece?

Available May 2007

More Brenda Adcock titles to watch for:

Reiko's Garden

Hatred...like love...knows no boundaries.

How much impact can one person have on a life?

When sixty-five-old Callie Owen returns to her rural childhood home in Eastern Tennessee to attend the funeral of a woman she hasn't seen in twenty years, she's forced to face the fears, heartache, and turbulent events that scarred both her body and her mind. Drawing strength from Jean, her partner of thirty years, and from their two grown children, Callie stays in the valley longer than she had anticipated and relives the years that changed her life forever.

In 1949, Japanese war bride Reiko Sanders came to Frost Valley, Tennessee with her soldier husband and infant son. Callie Owen was an inquisitive ten-year-old whose curiosity about the stranger drove her to disobey her father for just one peek at the woman who had become the subject of so much speculation. Despite Callie's fears, she soon finds that the exotic-looking woman is kind and caring, and the two forge a tentative, but secret friendship.

When Callie and her five brothers and sisters were left orphaned, Reiko provided emotional support to Callie. The bond between them continued to grow stronger until Callie left Frost Valley as a teenager, emotionally and physically scarred, vowing never to return and never to forgive.

It's not until Callie goes "home" that she allows herself to remember how Reiko influenced her life. Once and for all, can she face the terrible events of her past? Or will they come back to destroy all that she loves?

Available May 2007

Redress of Grievances

In the first of a series of psychological thrillers, Harriett Markham is a defense attorney in Austin, Texas, who lost everything eleven years earlier. She had been an associate with a Dallas firm and involved in an affair with a senior partner, Alexis Dunne. Harriett represented a rape/murder client named Jared Wilkes and got the charges dismissed on a technicality. When Wilkes committed a rape and murder after his release, Harriett was devastated. She resigned and moved to Austin, leaving everything behind, including her lover.

Despite lingering feelings for Alexis, Harriet becomes involved with a sex-offense investigator, Jessie Rains, a woman struggling with secrets of her own. Harriet thinks she might finally be happy, but then Alexis re-enters her life. She refers a case of multiple homicide allegedly committed by Sharon Taggart, a woman with no motive for the crimes. Harriett is creeped out by the brutal murders, but reluctantly agrees to handle the defense.

As Harriett's team prepares for trial, disturbing information comes to light. Sharon denies any involvement in the crimes, but the evidence against her seems overwhelming. Harriett is plunged into a case rife with twisty psychological motives, questionable sanity, and a client with a complex and disturbing life. Is she guilty or not? And will Harriet's legal defense bring about justice – or another Wilkes case?

Available August 2007

OTHER QUEST PUBLICATIONS

About the Author:

Originally from the Appalachian region of Eastern Tennessee, Brenda now lives in Central Texas, near Austin. She began writing in junior high school where she wrote an admittedly hokey western serial to entertain her friends. Completing her graduate studies in Eastern European history in 1971, she worked as a graphic artist, a public relations specialist for the military and a display advertising specialist until she finally had to admit that her mother might have been right and she earned her teaching certification. For the last twenty-plus years she has taught world history and political science. Brenda and her partner of ten years, Cheryl, are the parents of three grown children and one still in high school. They also have two grandchildren. Rounding out their home are three temperamental cats and an occasionally conscious Bassett Hound. When she is not writing Brenda creates stained glass and shoots pool at her favorite bar. She may be contacted at adcockb10@yahoo.com and welcomes all comments.

VISIT US ONLINE AT
www.regalcrest.biz

At the Regal Crest Website You'll Find

- The latest news about forthcoming titles and new releases

- Our complete backlist of romance, mystery, thriller and adventure titles

- Information about your favorite authors

- Current bestsellers

- Media tearsheets to print and take with you when you shop

Regal Crest titles are available from all progressive booksellers and online at StarCrossed Productions, (www.scp-inc.biz), or at www.amazon.com, www.bamm.com, www.barnesandnoble.com, and many others.